I0450860

Ignite the the Mountains

Kate Hall

Lost Window LLC

Copyright © 2019 Kate Hall

This paperback edition published 2019

Cover Art © 2019 EJ Chong

Published by Lost Window Publishing
Neosho, Missouri
United States

All rights reserved. No portion of this book may
be reproduced in any form without permission
from the publisher, except as permitted by U.S.
copyright law. For permissions contact:

LostWindowPublishing@gmail.com

ISBN: 978-1-950291-09-0

Jacket Design by Kate Hall
Jacket Art by EJ Chong

Interior Design by Kate Hall

"Above all, be the heroine of your life, not the victim."
Nora Ephron

Chapter One
Billie

THE DARK, HUMID AUDITORIUM IS LIKE an oven today, and everyone has been sweating for what feels like forever. Tom is being a dick, but that's nothing new. This afternoon, it's because he couldn't hit half the notes in his final song, and Ms. Nielsen isn't having it. He's sitting as far to the side of the stage as he can, his long legs stretched out in front of him with his mucked-up cowboy boots on the ground below instead of attached to his body. I feel bad for whoever is close enough to smell his feet.

I'm sitting in my usual place at center stage, my

short legs hanging over the edge and into the pit. Long before I ever even thought about acting, it used to be an orchestra pit, but this school's theatre program hasn't used a live orchestra in over a decade. Now it's mostly used for storage or hidden makeout sessions.

Not that I'd know anything about the latter.

Ms. Nielsen flips a page on her notebook and moves to sit in the front row, that way she's close enough that we can see the fire in her eyes as she reams us out for our terrible performance. The red velvet seats are like a cape flowing out behind her, the long-time queen of the theatre. Filicia, my best friend, is on her knees behind me, braiding my dull brown hair into a fishtail, a hairdo I've never been able to get right by myself.

She and I tried dating sophomore year, but she'd discovered she was aromantic and asexual, so we'd broken up rather quickly. We're still close as can be, though. Between us dating and breaking up, that has never changed. There's something about being neighbors our whole lives that has kept us close.

"Billie," Ms. Nielsen calls. I perk up and listen, straightening my shoulders in case she's getting onto me for slouching again. She looks pissed, but Ms. Nielsen always looks sort of pissed. That's just her face. "You need to work on walking in the heels. I want you to practice in them some more."

I sigh. I hate my ridiculous costume heels and tripped in them a dozen times tonight, but my blocking for Guinevere just doesn't work when I'm a foot shorter than Tom, who plays Arthur, and Greg, who plays Lancelot. It's not my fault country boys are bred tall and I'm, well, not. "No problem," I call back, putting both my thumbs up. It is a problem, but I would probably be eviscerated on the spot if I said as much. Ms. Nielsen is not known for showing mercy.

"Don't move," Filicia mumbles over the elastic in her mouth.

"Sorry," I reply.

Ms. Nielsen continues to go over her notes, and Tom, sitting at the far right of the stage, cringes every time she yells at him. She yells at everyone, though. That's just her voice. She's a loud person.

3

He should be used to it by now. It's not like he's any quieter. Just last week, he stood on his table and belted a country song in the middle of the cafeteria. For someone who's supposed to be a good singer, he'd done a terrible job.

The yellow legal pad is full, and every page flip is like a gunshot that makes the freshmen—and Tom—cringe. Behind us, volunteers from the meager art club are in the beginning stages of painting castle walls and flowers and other set pieces. The ancient canvas flats are lying across the stage floor, which will be painted with a fresh layer of pitch-black paint a few days before the show.

Just as Ms. Nielsen is finishing the legal pad, a girl I don't recognize walks in through the main auditorium doors.

Holy shit.

She's tall, taller than any of the other girls I know in Bore's Grove. And most people in Bore's Grove are tall, so that's really saying something. She's wearing a pair of skin-tight floral leggings and a black t-shirt, tight around her thick, toned biceps. Her blonde hair swings in a high ponytail as she strides through, everyone watching her, and she doesn't even care. I swallow, but my mouth is dry.

I don't even realize I'm staring until Filicia hisses, "Shut your damn mouth, Billie. You're embarrassing yourself."

I slam my mouth shut, but my eyes don't leave the incredible figure in front of me. It's like she's a magical warrior princess who appeared out of the forest and walked directly into our theatre rehearsal. She could probably dead-lift me without blinking. The girl goes up to Ms. Nielsen, who points her toward the stage after a brief conversation. Instead of taking the steps on either side, the girl walks in the pit and hops up onto the three-foot platform right next to me without even blinking. I can feel her warmth beside me, that's how close she is. When she makes eye contact with me, my cheeks heat.

Again, holy shit.

"Can we go now?" Tom asks. The interruption shakes me out of my stupor. Why does his voice have to ruin everything?

Ms. Nielsen waves her hand. "Yes, everyone can go. Except Tom. I'll see the rest of you on Monday." Friday rehearsals are always brutal since they're three hours long, but with broken conditioning, today had been extra horrible.

I glance over my shoulder, trying to be subtle as I look at the girl, but she's looking right back at me. A sly smile comes on her face, and I stumble off the stage toward Filicia's car. I look back one more time, but the girl has finally begun to paint, her eyes focused on the task ahead of her. Who is she?

"Her name is Theo," Filicia says after we go outside. Did she read my mind? I hadn't felt any sort of telepathic field in my head, but that doesn't mean much. I don't pay enough attention to that sort of thing, and I probably wouldn't notice if it were to happen. "Ms. Nielsen told me she'd be here. She's gonna be the prop master. Something we've never had before." Makes sense. Ms. Nielsen is always ready to give someone a job in the program so long as they're willing to work.

"Neat," I say, trying to sound casual. But really, I want to learn more about the mysterious Theo. I don't ask, though. I tend to come off as desperate and whiny.

Filicia rolls her eyes. We climb into her ancient Corolla, parts of which are taped on. Namely, the rear driver's side window. The car starts on the third try, practically a record for this thing. Filicia is the only one, between she, myself, and Kaylee, who owns a car at all, which means she's the designated chauffeur of our friend group.

We all work at the same diner, a chain that's installed in a truck stop off the interstate. The main customers are exhausted parents on a road trip with their young children and exhausted truck drivers. It's not glamorous work, but at least we don't get yelled at. Our customers are too sleep deprived for that.

Kaylee is already here when we arrive. Her mom dropped her off for her shift right after school ended at noon. Filicia and I go to the employee entrance in the back, and I give a half wave to one of the truck drivers whilst putting on my uniform button-up shirt and black apron outside. The moment we walk in, sounds of chaos envelope us.

"Eighty-six on onion rings," Kenneth, our manager, says in passing as Filicia and I clock in. We groan simultaneously. Four o'clock on a Friday is not the best time to run out of something so vital. The fry and burger grease is already sticking to my skin, and the hostess is putting someone in my section before I'm even done looking at the chart. Instead of my usual section full of booths, I mostly have tables tonight. Not many people choose tables, so I get to take care of eight people right off. Fantastic.

"Eighty-six on onion rings," I say to Ronnie, a tall Polynesian boy from my math class, as I rush to get drink orders.

As I'm writing them down, our hostess sits another large group in my section. This one is six people. I widen my eyes and stare at her, but she only shrugs, half-apologetic as she walks away. This must be because I got snippy with her for giving me three booths in a row last night. I grit my teeth and get the drink orders of the second table. Maybe I should say something to Kenneth.

Or maybe not. I don't want to cause a confrontation.

It's an agonizingly long evening. By six, I've already had far too many tables, and we're out of macaroni and cheese as well, much to the disdain of every five-year-old and their parents. Weekends are the absolute worst, but they're the only days I'm able to work during play season. My evenings are all tied up Monday through Thursday, so I get the long rushes every time.

When I have a moment to breathe, I finally make a run for it. "Smoke break," I call to the assistant manager as I slip out the back door.

"That shit'll kill you," he replies.

I collapse to the curb, stretching my legs out in front of me. I don't actually smoke, but it's a great way to get a five-minute break during an otherwise busy shift. The soles of my feet throb from the cheap non-slip shoes, and the air inside is nauseating. I half-wave at a Sikh truck driver as he passes me to go in through the commercial driver entrance at the back of the truck stop. Truck drivers don't tend to care when they see us lazing around for a minute or two, but if I were sitting in view of someone driving a car and parking at the front of the store, I'd be sure to get a complaint.

A squeak rouses my attention, and I turn my eyes to a pair of tiny faerie dragons that are fighting over an abandoned gas-station hot dog. Despite their miniscule sizes, they seem perfectly vicious. Neither of them is actually eating the probably rotten meal, as they're too busy snapping at each other, so I sneak over and grab it before they can. I then tear it in half and throw the pieces a few feet apart, catching their attention. The fight stops immediately as they hop over like birds for their prize.

I'm usually terrified of dragons, but these ones don't scare me nearly as bad. No, it's the enormous mountain dragons the size of a house that make me wary. The ones that can tear apart a town and ruin a little girl's life in one morning. The ones that can spurn her parents' divorce and give her nightmares of burning for years. It would've been less if we could afford therapy, but it's simply not in the budget.

My watch beeps to signify the end of my micro-break, and I stand, brushing any dirt and gravel off my cheap black slacks before going back inside. The thighs are already chaffing on these things, and I sigh. I'll have to buy new ones soon.

Instead of finding my customers happily munching on their dinners at their tables, everyone in the restaurant is against the East windows, their faces pressed up against the glass and fogging it up. Because of the oddity of the moment, it takes a few seconds for me to look up and notice what they're all starting at.

My breath catches, and my heart stops. An entire flock of mountain dragons is in the field just past the parking lot. The creatures are huge, taller than the building we stand in.

It's suddenly clear just how fragile this little pile of sticks really is. Does a building like this have an anti-fire spell over it? Or something to prevent us being crushed? They monsters are close enough to touch as one's wing hovers over the cars like they're ducklings and it's their mother. The creature turns its head, and its slitted golden eyes look directly into mine.

Blood drains out of my head. The ground is coming up too fast, and there's nobody near enough to catch me. Even if there was, they're all far too busy staring at the horror outside.

Chapter Two
Theo

THE THEATRE PROGRAM IS THE ONLY DECENT thing about this miserable school. Ms. Nielsen seems to know what she's talking about, and her Columbia Chicago degree isn't something to brush aside. It's not my old school, not even close, but at least I'll still have something to learn from her.

Mom doesn't know that I skipped class today. If she knew, I wouldn't have been allowed to join play practice this afternoon. I'm just on the crew, but I want to get on Ms. Nielsen's good side so I can potentially get a favorable role in the spring play. It's my senior year, and I need more credits for my college application and resumé.

I'd totally screwed up seeing the girl who clearly owns the auditorium, though. She'd been small and curvy, a stark contrast to my tall muscular figure. She'd just stared at me like I was some sort of freak, someone who shouldn't have had the audacity to walk into the building. She may be smaller than me, but I have no doubt that she could crush me underfoot with no problem. It must be why I'm so attracted to her.

After the actors all left, Ms. Nielsen had given me a copy of the script, although I'm quite familiar with Camelot. I have the soundtrack memorized, and I used to watch all the clips I could find of the original cast. Still, I went through and highlighted all the props and began to sort them out after helping with the backdrop. It had been interesting to listen to Ms. Nielsen instruct the guy playing Arthur, although I hadn't gotten his name.

When Mom picks me up in her orange Corvette, I remain silent. She's always saying that I annoy people by talking too much, so I've decided it's easier to just not talk at all.

She should just sell this car, the only thing she'd insisted on keeping after she left Dad. If she were really concerned about money, that would be the right thing to do. I don't say that out loud, though. She'll probably get annoyed by my voice.

"Any cute girls in your classes?" she probes, her voice teasing. Of course she's this way. Despite all her misgivings, she's still my embarrassing mom. Still, I don't want to talk to her. I will forever be bitter about being stuck in this town, and I won't let her tease a smile out of me. I turn my music up, letting Nina Rosario talk to me instead of her. Just breathe.

After another minute, Mom's voice seems insistent. I take one of my earbuds out and quirk an eyebrow at her.

"Do you want takeout, Theo?" she asks for what's probably the second or third time, clearly annoyed. But when isn't she annoyed with me?

"Depends. Do they even have takeout in the middle of nowhere?"

She sighs and ignores me, pulling out of the

school parking lot. After a brief search along the main strip and then a Google search from a bank's parking lot, it's clear that no, there is not takeout in Bore's Grove, Tennessee.

She settles on a place with a neon ice-cream cone on the sign and orders us bacon cheeseburgers and fries.

"And two chocolate shakes," she says to the intercom at the last second, glancing at me, and I roll my eyes.

The drive home is short–nothing is actually far around here. With a population of fifteen hundred, that's kind of impossible. And Nana's house is right in the middle of town. According to her, it's a local legend. The first house to be built, the origin of Bore's Grove. It was originally some rich guy's secluded country home, and the town was built years after it.

The house is a tall Victorian that is just starting to climb the mountain, its paint deceptively clean-cut blue and white. Nana wanted something cheery after grandpa died - well, after she killed him. Accidentally. Probably. The house is decidedly not haunted, which Nana had made sure of. I still refuse to go in the basement, though. It's not worth the risk.

I take my dinner and go up to my room, an airy space in the attic that is in desperate need of a remodel. Or at least some basic decor. The bed is a cheap particle-board twin placed under the window at the base of the sloped slat-board ceiling, so if I sit up too quickly in the morning, I hit my head. This morning, I'd hit it hard. The comforter and sheets are an old floral patterned set that Mom found still in its original plastic from the eighties, and I actually sort of like it. It's a decent vintage set, and if I could find matching furniture and decorations, the room would turn into a proper hipster retreat. My friends from the city would definitely make fun of me for it, although at least a few would be secretly jealous.

A knock, too light to belong to Mom, sounds at the door, and Nana enters without asking. She's a tall, lean woman, her athleticism not matching her age in the slightest. Her white hair is long and up in a girlish ponytail, and she's wearing tight jeans and a BeeJee's t-shirt. If not for the few wrinkles and tiny amount of loose skin, she could be my age with bleached hair. "I'm going to Knoxville tomorrow. I thought it could be a fun girls' trip. Find you something to bring some life into this attic." She eyes the foil burger wrapper abandoned on my bed, covered in ketchup drippings. "I think a trash can, perhaps?"

Around my crinkle-cut fries, I say, "That sounds fun. And I promise to bring my trash downstairs to throw it out tonight." A chunk of fry leaps out of my mouth and hits the hardwood floor on the last word, but Nana just snorts. I've always liked Nana more than Dad's parents, who are a snooty couple from the Hamptons and always make me wear overpriced dresses to their events.

"Be up by eight. I want to get good deals when the flea markets are putting out new stuff."

When I finish eating, I double task by simultaneously scrolling through Pinterest for room ideas and highlighting changes I want to make on a competitive acting piece I'd like to do next semester. Perhaps I should have at least shown up to that class instead of wandering town on foot. It would have been good to find out if I would even be able to find a tournament partner. Maybe the girl from rehearsal? I need to at least decide what events I'll compete in.

A shiver runs through me, and I shake my hands out, tiny blue sparks flying out and disappearing before they can ruin the sheets. I should really work on my practical magic, but I'd much rather practice acting. Even if I don't get to attend the performance art high school I'd been accepted to back in New York, I will do my best to keep it from affecting my future.

IRUN MY FINGERS OVER A WROUGHT-IRON bed frame, the flowers intricate and purposeful. This must have been crafted by hand by some sort of metal mage, subtle fingerprints still embedded in some parts of the flowers. I have no idea how something this gorgeous came to a flea market in Knoxville, Tennessee. The black Amex card burns a hole in my pocket, but a purchase like this would surely rouse suspicion. Mom knows I'm on Dad's side of the whole divorce, but she doesn't know that he got me a credit card before we left. She'd be pissed if she found out.

Nana is bartering with the stall owner over a white farmhouse-style sink. I don't see the point. There's already a perfectly fine stainless steel sink in the kitchen. I glance at the bed frame once again. I guess that, technically, I have a perfectly good bed in my room. I meander over to Nana, but not before pressing my finger against the cool metal at the center of one of the iron flowers. A faerie boy swerves far around me and the frame, eyeing it with venom.

I look over a pale pink armchair, sitting in it and resting my legs over the gold-painted wooden arm. It matches the color of the flowers on my bed-spread perfectly.

We continue through, and I catch Nana handing over cash more times than Mom might like. Mom is always worried that Nana is going to spend too much money, that she'll run out of her retirement savings. Now that I'm witnessing her spending habits firsthand, I can see why Mom might think that.

Eventually, when we run out of booths to peruse, we go out in the cool breeze toward the pickup truck and attached horse trailer that we picked up from an old man on the way out of town. Nana had obviously been prepared to do far too much shopping. A flock of prairie dragons is flitting under the truck, their golden-feathered tails sticking out in the sunshine as they hunt for coins and lost items for their nests. When Nana gets in the vehicle, they all scamper away at the noise of the doors, off to find another car to search under. A pair of boys my age meet us by the warehouse exit, and I scroll through Instagram while we wait for them to load Nana's purchases into the old gray horse trailer.

"I need to run into the bookstore while we're here," Nana says after a few minutes. I glance up from my phone to find that she's looking at me. How long have I been ignoring her gaze?

"That sounds fun," I say. "I wanted to find something for Interp for next semester." I've been scrolling through scripts and books online, but there's nothing quite like perusing a book store to help me find the perfect acting piece. I've also been itching to try out Dad's Amex card, and there's no place like a bookstore to have no spending limit.

Nana nods and pulls out of the lot after one of the boys hands her a receipt. I'm not looking forward to unloading all that furniture when we get home—I'm no good at household spells, so I'll probably end up carrying a bunch of stuff up to my room. I wish the flee market vendors had at least offered to teleport our purchases directly to the house, but I guess that's more of a New York thing. Or maybe just a mainstream furniture store thing.

The giant bookstore is a twenty minute drive, and I practically leap out of the truck the minute we pull in. Nana is surely behind me, but I go in the store before she can catch up, taking in a deep breath. The scent of new paper and coffee envelopes me, wrapping me up in its comfort. Yes, this is perfect.

I glance up to the second floor balcony, and there, looking right at me, is the girl from theatre.

Chapter Three
Billie

AFTER MY FAINTING INCIDENT, IT HAD BEEN tough to convince Dad to let me borrow his car to drive to Knoxville, but it had been worth the pleading. I hadn't even been injured, and, after a quick spell, the one doctor in Bore's Grove had convinced him there was nothing actually wrong with me.

I waste five precious dollars on a drink from Starbucks, and Kaylee goes off on her own the moment we walk into the bookstore. She's one of my best friends, and, because I've known her since we were toddlers, I know that she tends to need alone time after being around people for too long. I'll probably find her in a hidden nook in a few hours.

I wander up to the second floor, where they keep a good deal of the fiction section. Last year, I performed a rendition of Coraline as a humorous piece, and it had done really well. I would love to find something that does as well this year, although I'm still a little bitter that Filicia and Kaylee are doing a duo piece for the spring semester, leaving me without a partner.

I turn around to look over the balcony, and standing in the doorway, her face relaxed and blissful upon entering, is Theo.

She looks like a mythical creature, her blonde hair a halo around her. Instead of her form-fitting athletic clothes from yesterday, she's wearing a pair of vintage overalls with a black crop top underneath. The microscopic portion of skin below the shirt and above the waist of the overalls is agony. It takes me a moment to realize she's looking directly at me, and I smile and half-wave. My face heats by approximately a billion degrees upon the realization that she caught me staring.

She returns my smile, but her eyes are tight. Is her face turning red, too, or is that my imagination? She glances at the staircase and walks that way. Is she coming up to talk to me? What am I supposed to say to her when she gets here?

Too soon, she's standing in front of me, and I'm just as lost as I'd been when she arrived in the theatre yesterday.

"Hi," she says. "I'm Theo. I saw you at school yesterday? In theatre? I'm new."

I blanche. She's right in front of me, and she's so much taller than I first thought. She absolutely towers over me. I'd have to stand on my toes to kiss—

Oh, god, I'm staring. It's been far too long, and I'm just standing here. "Hi," I gasp out, thrusting my hand toward her. She smiles and takes it. Her hand is so soft. I don't want to let go. Thankfully, I don't make it even more awkward by holding on too long. When I let her hand go within the appropriate amount of time, I ask, "What are you doing here?"

I cringe at how rude my words sound. I've never been this nervous around anyone, not even Lucy Lawless when I met her at a convention last year.

Thankfully, she doesn't seem to take offense. "Oh, I'm just trying to find an interp piece. My grandma wanted to go to the flea market, and then we came here." Theo glances away and waves, and I turn in time to see an elderly woman with a long silver ponytail waving up at us.

I nod. "Me, too. I mean, looking for a piece. I want something fresh for the spring semester."

"What events are you doing?"

I shrug. "Just humorous for now. I've considered another dramatic piece, but I kind of hate it even though I'm doing one now. I'd like to do a duo, but I don't have a partner."

At that, her entire face lights up. "I would love to do a duo with you!"

The excitement on her face is blinding, and I have to look away. I have got to stop. I can already hear Filicia in my head calling me a useless lesbian, and of course she's right. I can't even have a two minute conversation with a pretty girl without getting totally flustered.

"I mean, we don't have to," Theo says, her tone more subdued. I look back at her, and her eyes are averted. Now, her face is definitely red. Bright red. Like mine must have been when she first walked in.

"No," I say, lifting my hands in front of me as if to touch her arms, but I freeze. "I mean, yes, that would be great. Did you do interp at your old school?"

Her smile returns. "Yeah. In New York. And I promise I'm not bad at it. I got third at national districts last year, and fifth at state."

"That's kind of amazing. I imagine there's a lot of talent up in New York." Is this flirting? Is this how flirting works? I have no idea. Thankfully, Kaylee walks up at that exact moment.

"Hey, Billie, do you think The Witches would make a good piece? I know someone did it at nationals once but it's been quite a while," she says, eyes on the book in her hand. When she looks up at me, then to Theo, a slow smile spreads over her face. "Oh. Who's this?"

Before I can answer, Theo sticks out her hand.

"Theo. I'm new in Bore's Grove. We were just talking about doing a duo this spring."

At her name, Kaylee gives me one of her looks. The kind of look that says, We will be talking about this later. Of course Filicia has mentioned Theo's appearance to her. At least Theo doesn't seem to notice the significant look Kaylee is giving me. "Well, we're excited to have you. The team could always use new people. And I know Billie was looking for a partner."

The double meaning brings heat into my face.

"Maybe we should look for pieces," I say. "It could take a while. And yeah, Kaylee, I think The Witches could work."

With that, Kaylee abandons us. She's definitely doing this on purpose. I haven't had a romantic partner in a long time, and she and Filicia tend to get the brunt of my complaints about that fact.

Theo and I stand far enough apart to be polite, and I try to avoid glancing at her as she squats to look at the lower shelves. She's probably not even interested in girls, although I do notice that the hems of her overalls are cuffed. It could just be a fashion statement, but it could be a subtle gay signal.

Doesn't matter.

Still, I ask, "So, how's New York? I've never been, but I'm looking at colleges there." This isn't technically true. I have scrolled obsessively through the NYU website, but there's no way I can afford it or even hope to get into their theatre program. I'm going to get my two-year deisel technician degree and get a job working on semi trucks. The pay is good, which is all that matters. That's what I tell myself, anyway.

"Oh, it's great," she says. "I mean, it's terrible, but that's part of the charm. Last month, a rat stole an entire sandwich out of my hand on the subway."

"Ugh," I say. "Sounds amazing."

She laughs. "But really. It's great. I grew up there. You can always get takeout, even if it's four in the morning."

I nod. The only thing you can get at four in the morning in Bore's Grove is something greasy from my diner. We don't even have a Walmart. "I'm sure that dating is a lot easier there, too. There are, like, ten people that are even mildly dateable here."

She purses her lips, and I think it's at my comment until I realize she's just reading the back cover of a book. "Yeah. My last girlfriend lived two floors down from me."

Girlfriend. My heart soars, although I rationalize that there's no way someone like her would be interested in someone like me. Why would a rich city girl want to hang out with a poor, hopeless case like me?

"I mean, the last girl I dated lives in my trailer park." I might as well rip off that bandaid now. If she has a problem with me being poor, I don't want anything to do with her.

She sets the book back on the shelf and then stands, shaking her feet out as she towers over me. "Isn't it weird? Living right by an ex? I ended up taking the stairs for like a month after we broke up. I lived on the twelfth floor."

I laugh. "It's not so bad. Filicia is ace, so it's not like we had a bad falling out. She's in theatre, too. Technician."

We go on talking like this, and the time slips

by like a stream. Before I know it, the sky outside has gone dark, and a voice says over the intercom, "The store will be closing in fifteen minutes."

"Jesus," I mutter, checking the time on my phone. At this point, Theo is holding an entire stack of books. I'd offered to take half, but she'd refused, pointing out that she lifts weights and doesn't mind. "I guess we've gotta go."

"I'll get these," Theo says. I begin to protest, but she stops me. "My dad gives me an allowance. It's really no problem."

I shrug. I can't really afford the expense, so I don't argue further. She leaves me on the second floor, and I find Kaylee reading a young adult novel in one of the plush armchairs. There's another book in front of her, the first book to the sequel in her hands. How did we stay here for so long? "Time to go," I say, tapping her on the shoulder. She yawns and stretches before we make our way to the front.

After she pays, we go outside, and I catch Theo's eye. Her grandma mutters something, and she looks away, a delicate smile on her lips.

Kaylee nudges me, and we climb into Dad's Ford Explorer. Hope blooms in my chest, and I smile as I start the SUV.

Chapter Four
Theo

THE WEEK IS LONG, AND I HATE MOST OF my classes. On the bright side, my final class of the day is Interp, also known as "Oral Interpretation of Literature," and I get to sit with Billie to work on our spring pieces. After school, I have to work hard to avoid Mom's probing questions. I do not want to speak with her, and that's that.

My room is a lot more homey. Nana bought me the pink armchair and a gold and glass desk, so I feel a lot more welcome when I get home. It's no longer a dusty guest bedroom, but my own space.

Halfway through the week, during play rehearsal, Ms. Nielsen asks if I'll be going to the Dragon's Day parade, and I agree to attend. I already know the song, after all.

When the morning of the parade comes, we all meet at the park in our costumes, although some students don't have their hair and makeup done yet. My costume from the depths of the costume closet isn't totally coordinated with everyone else's, and the skirt is too short, but I make it work. I'm glad to just be involved. I straighten my flower crown, one of the half dozen that the performing girls are wearing.

"It's gonna be fine," Kaylee says to Billie, whose face is stricken. "They cross every year, and nothing has happened."

I tilt my head, then lean over to Filicia, who I've spoken to quite a bit at rehearsal throughout the week, as we're both backstage all afternoon. "What's going on?"

Filicia is doing someone's hair, one of the freshman girls. "There's supposed to be a flock of mountain dragons passing by town during the parade. It freaks a lot of people out, mainly because of the one that destroyed town five years ago."

My mouth pops open. I'd forgotten all about that, and now the memory of Mom desperately trying to contact Nana rushes back to me. That's what the parade is for. I can't believe I didn't make the connection until now. "And Billie?"

Filicia talks over a pin that's in her mouth. "Billie saw it all happen. She'd run away from home because of her parents' divorce, and she made it to the top of the mountain by the time the dragon came down. It was two days before she was found in the woods and reunited with her family. She thought they all died."

"Holy shit," I breathe. "That must have been awful."

Filicia nods. "Yeah. Dragons really freak her out."

I don't respond, but I'm careful around Billie all evening. She's wearing a floor-length blue dress with fake flowers at the base of the tulle skirt, a unique take on Julie Andrews' original dress from the Broadway show. Her hair comes down in waves over the puffy tulle sleeves. She really does look like a queen, but her eyes keep darting to the sky above us.

When Tom shows up last, he has a cocky grin on his face. "Guess what I brought," he says, and a few of the other students go to join him. He pulls a sword out of a leather sheath. It looks sharp. "It's real, too. My cousin does renaissance festivals and shit, and he said I could borrow it."

"Isn't that dangerous?" I call, crossing my arms over my chest.

He sheaths it again. "Not if I have it."

Somehow, I doubt that. Nielsen calls for everyone to get in position, though, and Tom and Billie climb on the float together, along with Greg, the boy playing Lancelot. Everyone else will be on the ground, dancing and handing out candy to children. This is all a very interesting way to commemorate a dragon attack. Interesting, of course, doesn't always mean good, but I say nothing. It's not my place.

We're the very first float, apparently quite the honor. The instrumentals play over a jukebox, and Billie has a microphone to sing the lead vocals for

"The Lusty Month of May," a fun and scandalous pick for a small town parade. It's the most upbeat of all the songs, and the only one where her costume is ready, so it was really the best option.

Her face alights when she's acting, and she definitely outshines Tom and Greg, kind of like the sun outshines a waning candle. I can't keep my eyes off her.

The parade is long and slow, and I'm completely exhausted by the time we reach the final stretch toward the square. I can just make out the fountain at the center of the patch of grass when a glass shriek slices through everything. The blood runs cold in my bones.

I've never heard a dragon's scream in person, but there's no mistaking it.

Just as someone turns off the radio and the pickup truck pulling our float stops at the square, a creature that's too big to possibly exist plummets to the earth. Its red scales glisten in the street lights, and its chest glows gold as it prepares a blast of fire. It's standing so close that I can see the subtle pearlescent glisten of its teeth, the shine of saliva that slowly evaporates as the temperature rises in the back of its throat.

The creature looks directly at me, a deep rumble reverberating out of its chest. I am nothing. I am small, a mouse in the eyes of a hawk. I am a seal being pursued by an orca whale. It is the predator, and I am its prey.

It takes a step back.

I am going to die.

Chapter Five
Billie

WHEN I WAS IN MIDDLE SCHOOL, I would watch a ton of nature documentaries. I was especially interested in the ones with dragons, and I was the kid who rooted for the dragon to catch the terrified deer. The predator had to eat, too, and, to me, dragons were incredible creatures. When I had to stand and watch my life, my town, my home get destroyed by the flames of a mountain dragon, I stopped watching that kind of stuff. It had been too hard to root for the same creatures that had ruined everything.

The main thing I remember from those documentaries, though, is how the prey animal would always react to the dragons. There was always a moment where it would freeze. I used to wonder why the deer or whatever didn't run. Didn't it know it was going to die? But then, when they did run, they still stood no chance. Not against the perfect predator. Especially not after it spent so much of its precious time frozen with fear.

Now, I get it. The hot scales are close enough that I can feel the warmth penetrate my gown, and everyone is just standing around, staring. Tom's hand is frozen just above the hilt of his sword, the one he'd been bragging about less than an hour ago, and the dragon is there in front of us, its teeth bared and flames building in its throat.

And in front of it, frozen with eyes wide, is Theo. Beautiful, mysterious, strong Theo, directly in the path of its flames.

I don't even think. The next eight seconds happen in flashes, like a strobe light.

Flash. I'm yanking Tom's sword out of its sheath. I half expect it to make a shing sound, like in the movies, but it doesn't.

Flash. I'm leaping off the float, my dress floating around me as though I'm flying. My hair whips in my face, and I have to shake it off when I hit the ground, a dull pain ricocheting through my feet and up my legs.

Flash. I'm running, faster than I've ever run. I shove Theo out of the way. She never even saw me coming.

Flash. The dragon is upon me. Its teeth are so close that I can smell its rotten breath, composed of cooked meat and sick teeth.

Flash. As though I'm possessed, I plunge the sword upwards, the blade slicing through the meat of the dragon's chin far too easily. It goes all the way up to the hilt, barely catching on the bone that's not doing well enough to protect its cranium.

I fall back when I yank the sword out, collapsing to the ground at the same time as the dragon. It's like it's all happening in slow motion. This monster is falling around me, and everyone is screaming and running. This must be a dream. Nothing about this moment could possibly be real, right?

Hot blood sticks to my skin, red as fire.

Someone's arms wrap around me, and I turn to see Theo lifting me before running. I look back to where I'd just been on the ground, and the claw at the apex of the dragon's enormous wing digs into the soft earth.

That could have been me.

The sword clatters to the pavement, and my legs are shaky when Theo sets me down.

I open my mouth, then close it. She doesn't say anything, and we both turn to stare at the dead mountain dragon on the ground.

"Billie," a voice yells from the sidelines. I turn, and Dad is pushing through the scrambling bodies. He's taller than most people, so he stands out, and he runs forward. Doris, my twelve-year-old sister, is right on his tail. If she weren't so good with her elbows, someone would have plowed down her meager frame by now.

Dad rushes to me and wraps me in a hug. He smells like aftershave and home, and a shudder runs through me.

I could have died.

I almost did.

A sob rips out of me.

"You're alright," he says, patting my head. "It's gonna be fine."

By the time the police arrive, I'm sitting on the float between Dad and Doris, and Theo is off to the side with her mom, a tall woman with severe features. Why is everyone in this town so tall? The thought shouldn't matter, but when I feel like I'm the only short person in town, it does.

I answer all the questions I'm asked, although it's hard to focus with the dead dragon lying right there. Theo is being questioned as well, and I notice her gesture toward me more than once. I want to go to her, to make sure she's truly okay, that she isn't upset or just completely traumatized. I am surprisingly fine, my mind calm and collected.

Despite the cool evening, the long dress I'm wearing is starting to get hot. I roll up the sleeves, but it doesn't really help.

Finally, the officer questioning me dismisses me and my family.

"Let's go home, kiddo," Dad says, putting a

hand on my shoulder to steer me toward his old SUV, which he's parked in the lot behind the courthouse off the square. I pad after him, but not before taking one last look at Theo, whose eyes are haunted as she stares after me, her lips in a thin, tight line.

I don't know how, but tonight has changed everything.

Chapter Six
Theo

IT'S TOO QUIET WHEN WE PULL INTO THE driveway. After all the noise and calamity at the parade, the silence is absolutely deafening. Still, when Mom opens her mouth to speak, I clamber out of the car. I don't want to talk about what happened, especially not with her. I'm exhausted from talking to the police, and all I want is to be alone to process the evening.

The air is cool and tinged with the scent of pine, and I take a deep breath in and walk around the back of the house instead of going inside and up to my room. I can't be around anybody right now.

Too much has happened.

Somewhere in the neighborhood, a dog barks, and I clutch that sound like a lifeline. Normal. It's so, so normal. The gate to the back yard is tall and wooden like the rest of the fence, and a splinter stings into my finger when I try to open it. I hiss and pull my hand back, squinting to look for the offending bit of wood, but it's too dark. In New York, it was never this dark, not anywhere. Even in town, though, Bore's Grove goes nearly black at night. I shove the gate open and march to the back porch, sitting on the ancient wooden steps that Nana built.

A shiver rips through me, but there is no breeze. It's not even that chilly out, although the autumn season is getting late. I'm still wearing my costume, though, which I'm supposed to return on Monday in Interp class. I wrap my arms around my waist and lean forward, resting my forehead on my knees. I suck in a breath, and another shiver runs through me, goose pimples rising on my flesh.

I'm alive.

I'm alive I'm alive I'm —

A splash interrupts my spiraling thoughts, and I jerk my head up. I can just make out the shape of Nana's above-ground pool, which has been covered and mostly drained for the season. I stare at the dim shape in the backyard, but nothing else happens.

I must have imagined it.

I pull out my phone, my hands shaking, and I look up Wendy's Instagram profile.

I shouldn't be torturing myself like this, but I scroll through my ex-girlfriend's profile anyway. There isn't anything new up, but I have to refresh the page a few times before I accept that there is, in fact, something different.

All the pictures of me are gone.

I drop the phone on the step next to me and rest my face in my hands. It doesn't even make sense that Wendy broke up with me. I mean, sure, I'd moved. But I'll be back in the city in May, the moment I graduate. Two years is an awful lot to throw away just because of a few months of distance. I suck in a shaky breath, and then blow it out as tears prick at my eyes.

Before they can fall, though, another splash slices into my senses. I groan and stand up, grabbing my phone off the step. I close out of the app without looking at it, then turn on the flashlight function. By the time I reach the pool, I consider that I should maybe have a weapon in case a murderous meth dealer is hiding out in Nana's pool.

I glance around and grab the pool skimmer off the hooks in the fence. It will have to do.

I shine my light on the pool and almost immediately spot the tear in the lining. Definitely not big enough for a meth dealer to go through. But it might be big enough for a rabid raccoon. Or a baby bear. I do a quick glance around, but I don't see a mother bear hiding in the darkness.

I carefully unhook the tarp that covers the pool, moving my phone to my mouth so I can unhook the cover with one hand and grip the skimmer with the other. If a rabid raccoon does jump at me, I want something to use to swat it away. The net doesn't seem all too sturdy, but I don't think about it too much. If I can survive a dragon attack, I can protect myself from a raccoon.

When I toss the tarp back, though, nothing is there. I squint to the far end of the pool, but I can't make out anything but half a foot of water. Another splash, and I look straight down.

It's not a raccoon.

The creature is slick and pathetic and smaller than I expect, but it's very clearly a dragon. More specifically, a baby mountain dragon. I glance to the sky, expecting to be attacked at any moment, but nothing comes. When I look back down, the baby flaps its wings and claws at the thick pool liner, but nothing happens other than the creature splashing back down into the water that's just shallow enough for it to avoid drowning.

Maybe I should let it drown.

I shake away the thought, though, and use the pool skimmer. The dragon startles away, hissing at the strange new object coming toward it.

"It's okay," I whisper around the phone in my mouth. "I'm trying to help you."

When I move the skimmer toward it again, though, it falls backward, its head plummeting into the icy water. I sigh and drop the skimmer on the dying autumn grass, then turn my phone's light off before placing it on the ground next to the skimmer. There's only one way for this to happen, and I'm not going to enjoy it one bit.

I huff and pull myself up over the edge. The ladder is around the other side of the pool, so I'd have to take the tarp off completely to access it. It's so much easier to just lift myself over the edge of the pool. The moment my feet plummet into the icy water, though, I suck in a breath and my feet sting.

"Fuck," I whisper, balling my hands into fists.

I expect the dragon to splash away from me, but instead, it immediately hops onto my costume dress, burrowing its claws in as it climbs up. I bite my tongue to avoid yelling out when the tiny claws dig into my skin. Instead, I gather the soaked hem of the skirt and pull it up, wrapping the dragon up.

"Please don't set me on fire," I mumble, clutching the dragon to my stomach and showing my costume pantaloons to the dark world around me. I expect its body to be hot against mine, but instead, it's like holding a block of ice. That can't be good. How long has it been in this pool?

I think back to the parade, to the dragon screeching and falling from the sky. Had it been his mother?

I heave myself back out of the pool, careful not to press the dragon against the cool metal. This is a lot harder now that I can only use one hand.

I tumble out of the pool, the hem of my skirt making a horrible ripping sound that I'm sure I'll hear about on Monday when I return the costume. Maybe I can convince Ms. Nielsen that it happened at the parade?

The dragon in my dress chirps, and I pull the hem out to see its golden eyes staring up at me. Its body trembles, and I hold it closer, wrapping it in my arms to try to give it some semblance of warmth. I carefully pull the tarp back down and put away the skimmer before grabbing my phone to go inside.

When I creep in the back door, Mom and Nana's voices float through the kitchen from the living room. I can't understand their words, but their tones indicate that they're arguing about something. If I'm fast, I can sneak around the corner and up the stairs.

I make it all the way to the third step before their voices stop.

"Theo?" Mom calls, her voice careful. "Are you alright?"

I roll my eyes. She saw me not twenty minutes ago. What could have possibly happened in that time to make her think I'm less okay than I was on the drive home? I glance at the pouch I've made out of my skirt as if to answer my own question.

"Yeah," I call back. "I think I'm just gonna read for a bit before I go to bed. Take some time for myself." This is more words than I've said to Mom the whole time we've been in Bore's Grove, and I hope she doesn't notice. Is my voice too high?

There's a pause, but she doesn't push the issue. "Let me know if you need anything, okay?"

I sigh with relief. "I will."

I lock myself in my room, and by the time I'm sitting on the bed, the dragon's eyes are closed, and it doesn't respond to my movement. If it doesn't warm up fast, it's going to die.

I keep my hands on the tiny creature, bundling its wings together against its body. It's no bigger than a dachshund, so it must be pretty young. I close my eyes and concentrate on the electricity running through me, a magic that I keep hidden in the darkest, deepest parts of my body. I don't let it escape, instead allowing it to run just below the skin of my hands so that I can warm up the baby.

The change is immediate. The dragon sucks in a ragged breath, and its eyes open to look up at me. I have to hold it for a few minutes before it begins to move again, though.

Now that I have it in my room, though, I wonder.

What am I supposed to do with a dragon?

Chapter Seven
Billie

IT'S MISERABLE AND RAINING OUTSIDE, and inside, it smells like wet dog. Einstein, our golden retriever, rests his head on my lap, whining if I stop petting him for even a moment. We've had him since I was in second grade, so I'm used to doing homework with one hand by now.

"What's up, asshole?" Doris asks.

My gaze darts up from my laptop to my little sister, who's wearing a flat cap with her hair tucked under it. I don't ask where she got it. "Language," I chastise. Ever since she started puberty, she's become a bit of a dick.

She rolls her eyes. "You say it all the time."

I prick an eyebrow at her. "I'm also eighteen years old."

She sighs and sits down at the table. Although it's late afternoon, she's still wearing her Doctor Who pajamas. "You get to do everything," she mumbles, propping her chin on her hands, squishing her cheeks in the process.

I ignore her and go back to my homework, but she sighs melodramatically.

"Did you need something?" I ask, my voice clipped.

"I want to go to Mom's," she whines. "There's nothing to do here."

"There's nothing to do at Mom's either," I point out. Lately, Doris has been talking a lot about spending time with Mom, who makes very little effort to spend time with us ever since she moved to Gatlinburg.

"She could bring me to the aquarium," Doris counters.

"She's not supposed to bring people with her all the time. And if you want to go over there, call her and have her pick you up."

A frustrated sound comes out of Doris, and she shoves away from the table. "You're the worst, you know that? You don't even like Mom!"

"Probably because she's a homophobe," I mumble. Half the reason she left was because of the dragon attack, but the other was because Dad came out shortly after. Ever since then, Mom has done nothing but talk shit about him. Usually using slurs. So it's not like I can risk coming out to her anytime soon.

Doris doesn't hear me, as she's already halfway to her room. The slam of the door shakes the house, and Einstein jerks his head up, his ears pricked toward the hallway.

"Hormones," I explain to the dog.

I hit print on my finally finished essay. There's a speech and debate tournament on Friday, so I have to get all my assignments done in advance. At least this was the only thing needed for this week.

After an hour of doing practice problems, I set down my notebook and sigh at my laptop. I've been putting off my college application for a month now, although there's no reason for it. I have a pretty good grade point average, and it's not like I'm applying to Columbia University, which is sixty grand before room and board. I'm going to Bore's Grove Tech, a tiny school with a decent mechanic program. If I get in, I can drive to school or hitch a ride with any of the half-dozen other students going in my neighborhood alone.

The application takes ten whole minutes, half of which is just trying to figure out how to send my FAFSA. I decide that it probably just goes to the "Financial Aid" department, and I hit submit.

As I change from the financial aid site to Twitter, the back door opens, and Dad walks in. His park ranger uniform is absolutely soaked, and he tosses his hat on the kitchen counter.

"Long day?" I ask, raising an eyebrow at the hat. I just cleaned the kitchen this morning whilst avoiding my assignments.

He notices my pointed glance and picks up the hat, hanging it on the hook by the door instead. Where it belongs. Good.

He runs his hand over his short beard and then

behind his neck. "Wet day," he says. "Some lady said her cat escaped her RV."

"Sounds like fun," I say. "Did you find the cat?"

He shakes his head. "No, turns out it was just hiding in the bathroom cabinet. Which we only found out after two hours of searching around the campsite."

I shouldn't laugh, because the situation sounds miserable, but I can't help myself. Dad is always getting into these types of overly helpful predicaments.

His blue eyes, the same ones Doris has, flick to the window as a crash of thunder shakes the house. Sometimes I wish I looked more like Dad, too, but my genes are more along line with my mom's. At least Doris has a lot working for her. Maybe she'll get his personality as she gets older, too. "Glad to be home, though." He kisses me on top of my head as he walks past toward the fridge. "Have you girls eaten yet?" When he opens it, I glimpse at the emptiness. We almost never cook, mainly because Dad is always at work, I'm too busy with homework, and Doris just doesn't want to try.

I shake my head. "I was thinking about ordering a pizza."

He nods absently. "Probably a good idea."

I look back at my laptop, chewing my bottom lip.

"Can I skip school tomorrow?" I ask. "You know, because of all the trauma?"

When I turn back to look at Dad, he seems skeptical at my tone. "Sure you can," he surprises me by saying. Just as I'm about to sigh with relief, he says, "but if you stay home, you'll have to miss rehearsal."

Damn it.

"Ugh. Fine. But I hope someone else has an escaped cat," I say.

He tilts his head and pauses. "How are you doing? After last night? I mean, really?"

Dad is always so concerned about us. It pisses me off that Doris is so hung up on our deadbeat mother when Dad tries so hard every day, working his ass off to make sure we have everything he can give us. It's like she has to prove something to Mom to make sure she still loves us.

"I'm okay," I lie. I don't mention that I didn't sleep last night. He doesn't need to be more worried than he already is. "I think I've kind of repressed it already. I'll tell you in a decade when I need therapy." The joke is to lighten the mood, but it takes him a minute to respond.

He gives a half smile, but his eyes are exhausted. "Alright, sweetie. Do you want to call for pizza and I'll go pick it up? No reason to make Landon deliver all the way out here in this weather." The pizza place in town, Gino's, is locally owned, and Landon is their only delivery boy. He's lived three streets down from us since I was a toddler. I'm pretty sure he was in the crowd at the parade last night, but it's hard to remember with everything else that happened.

I call and order the food, glancing out the window warily as a small flock of prairie dragons lands in the neighbor's patch of autumn-yellowed grass. They huddle under the house's small porch, and I close the blinds and go to my room to wait for Dad to get the pizza.

I can't wait for this stupid migration season to

be over. Then, I can get back to my life.

Chapter Eight
Theo

I DON'T SHARE ANY CLASSES WITH BILLIE aside from Interp, so I have to wait for the end of the day to see her. Still, I've caught glimpses of her in the halls and the cafeteria, usually chatting with other students as they approach her.

When I walk in the room, though, Tom is sitting in my seat, a barrage of questions spouting out. I take the desk in front of her instead, but she doesn't acknowledge me. How do you talk to someone about the fact that they saved your life? Or the fact that you've got an illegal mountain dragon in a makeshift enclosure in your bedroom?

I open my laptop and begin typing at our spring duo piece without consulting her about it. What if she doesn't want to do a piece with me anymore?

Nielsen is sitting at her desk at the front of the room, her sewing machine running. It appears that she's making some sort of tunic, probably for Tom's King Arthur costume, which hadn't been finished in time for the parade. I shudder at the memory of the parade, pushing it out of my mind as swiftly as it arrived. It's easier not to think about it.

After the bell rings to announce the start of class, Tom moves off to practice his piece. Just as I'm about to gain the courage to twist around in my seat to talk to Billie, Nielsen calls my name. I sigh, perhaps with indignation, perhaps with relief. I'd like to tell myself it's the former, but the tension easing out of my shoulders tells me otherwise.

"What's up?" I ask when I approach the formidable heavy wooden desk.

"Do you have a piece?" she asks, not even bothering to look at me.

"I...what?"

She continues. "Someone dropped out of the

tournament this weekend and I need a dramatic piece to fill the slot."

It takes me a moment to process what she's actually asking. "I mean...Yeah. Yes. I do."

I can feel the grin spreading across my face, but Nielsen doesn't smile back. I should be embarrassed, but I'm alight with giddiness. With the play being long cast, I haven't had a chance to do any real acting since New York. When I get to my seat, I immediately open the file on my laptop to re-read it and refresh it.

I mumble the words, getting into the head of my character, a mother whose child was killed by a technical issue in her vehicle. I read it over and over again even though I memorized it weeks ago, and then I close my laptop most of the way and mumble the words, giving myself a moment after stumbling to remember before checking the script.

By the time I remember that I wanted to speak to Billie, the final bell of the day rings, and class is over.

Chapter Nine
Theo

FOR THE REST OF THE WEEK, BILLIE doesn't speak to me. I try to start conversations with her, but I can never find the right words to say. It's not like I can say "Thanks for saving my life, but I have the baby of the dragon you killed in my room."

During rehearsal, when I'm not needed backstage —which, to be honest, is most of the time— I'm rehearsing my dramatic acting piece, facing the wall and mouthing the words. I'm more bold about it in class, speaking the words aloud, but Nielsen would probably murder me if she heard a peep backstage during play rehearsal. It has to be perfect. I can't let this opportunity slip away.

Still, entrenched as I am in my piece, I notice things. My eyes meet Billie's more times than I can count as she's coming off stage. Her gaze burns at the back of my neck in class as I rehearse, but by the time I finish to turn to her, she's staring at the wall and rehearsing her own. Back home, I dwell on it, all the while keeping my own secret.

I am entranced by Billie on stage every time. Although she's not in her costume, she is Guinevere more than anyone has ever been. Her sorrow at marrying a man she's never met, her desperate love for Lancelot, her quiet resignation at being burned at the stake…It's all there, and if I look, I'm trapped in her performance. What I wouldn't give to be Lancelot for just an instant.

I keep these thoughts especially close. It's probably just a savior complex. Meaningless. There's no reason to bother Billie with this crush.

Ugh. I hate having crushes.

On Thursday night, I'm packing for the tournament with the dragon perched on my shoulder when Nana barges in without knocking.

"When did you intend to tell me that you were keeping a dragon in my house?" she asks. Her voice is surprisingly calm, but her eyebrows are practically to her hairline.

The dragon, whom I haven't named so I theoretically don't get attached, scurries away into the little magic heat bubble I made for him, hissing and flaring his wings out to make himself look bigger than a cat. It's not very effective.

"Um," I answer brilliantly.

Nana strides over and kneels down. She never fails to surprise me with how limber she is for her age. Instead of cooing or talking, when the dragon hisses, she hisses back. This seems to throw him, as he drops his wings and tilts his head.

"What's his name?" she asks.

I shrug even though she's not looking at me. "I wasn't gonna give him one."

Nana squints, and the dragon leans forward and sniffs at her. "I like Maximus."

"Like the horse in Tangled?"

She nods. "Yeah. It was on TV today."

I sigh. "I mean, obviously we have to find a rescue. Or a sanctuary. Or something."

Nana shrugs. She doesn't seem very pressed about what should be a very serious situation. "I think we should see how this plays out."

That doesn't even make any sense. Is she finally going senile? I didn't think it ran in the family, but you can never be sure. She should absolutely know that this is illegal, and she should in no way be encouraging me to actually keep a dragon in the house.

I tap my hands on my leggings impatiently. "So, this may be the wrong time to ask, but can you watch him while I'm at the tournament? He needs to eat every three hours." I bite my lip so that I don't end up rambling.

Instead of answering, Nana just sort of flaps her hand at me. She's completely enraptured by Maximus, a smile in her eyes even though there isn't one on her lips.

Well, at least there's someone on my side.

Chapter Ten
Theo

DEBATE TOURNAMENTS IN THE MID-WEST are no different than they had been in New York. Most of the tournament is reserved for actual rounds of debate, so those of us who only compete in interpretive events end up sitting around most of the tournament. I use most of this time to look up baby dragon videos on YouTube, although I spend a little time conversing with Kaylee in the cafeteria where we're based.

Although I'm out of practice, I manage to make the final round with my dramatic piece. Billie's number is also on the chart, but she's also competing in the finals of the Humorous event, so she goes to a different classroom. I'm the first up for the round, and I take a deep breath and write my information on the board as the judges finish getting ready. My palms sweat, and the marker becomes a bit too moist for my liking.

When I stand at the front of the room, though, waiting for the three judges to let me know they're ready, everything else fades away. As soon as I begin my piece, I am no longer Theo, New York disaster in a small town. I'm a woman whose child has just died, a woman seeking justice for the untimely death of her son due to the car's brake failure.

As it has always been with dramatic pieces, the clapping is subdued when I finish my piece. I take a seat at the back of the room to watch the rest of the round.

There are a couple of pretty good pieces and one really bad one that doesn't make sense being in the round. The fifth competitor is just okay, and then Billie walks in when they finish.

She's wearing her debate suit, a pair of black slim-cut trousers with a blush pink shirt and black blazer. Despite being at the tournament all day, her hair is still in a perfect bun, and her makeup looks just as new as when I saw her in the hotel at six-thirty this morning. How does she do it? I'm certain I'm a mess.

The moment she transforms for her piece, it's over for me. Hers is about a woman who's being cheated on and gaslighted by her husband only to end up institutionalized. Just like in play rehearsal, she doesn't just play the character, she becomes her. She is no longer Billie, but a woman scorned. A woman driven to illness and locked away.

As she completes the piece, it's like the entire room is holding its breath. One of the judges, a college student with at least six piercings, has tears streaming down his face.

It takes a moment for the usual subdued clapping, but she definitely gets more of it than anybody else in the round had. We all filter out so that the judges can fill out their paperwork. She surely got the top spot, the coveted "One." I attended a private school for some of the most skilled student actors in New York, and she could have blown any one of them out of the water.

After the quarter-final debate rounds comes the award ceremony, and Billie and I stand together, hands clenched as they call out awards even though we haven't spoken all week. We're the last two on stage, and Billie hugs me and beams as I'm given the second place trophy. Our entire team stands to clap as we're given our first and second place trophies, and I grin.

She wins first in Humorous, as well, which means she's gotten the best awards of anyone at our school. Kaylee got fifth in Poetry, and Tom got fourth in Humorous.

We clamber toward the bus, and the Interpers — and a few of the debaters — gush at Billie. I hang back and smile, getting the occasional smile and pat on the back for my second place trophy.

I'm one of the first on the bus, and I have an entire seat to myself. I would do anything to sleep the entire two and a half hour drive home. Between getting up at five in the morning and eating garbage food all weekend, I'm absolutely exhausted. Still, when Billie takes the seat across from mine, I sit up a little straighter and smile at her.

Tentatively, she smiles back.

"Congrats on your trophies," I say. It's simple, the easiest of conversation starters.

"You too," she replies.

At that, Nielsen climbs on the bus and does a quick roll-call to make sure everyone not staying for the final rounds of debate are ready to go. Within moments, the lights are out and the bus is moving. Time to get out of this tournament bubble and head home.

I lean my head back, staring out at the lights as the bus rolls out of town. Just as I'm getting my earbuds out, Billie's voice catches my attention. "Are you gonna be at more tournaments this semester?"

I turn to her, only to see that she's taken her dark hair down from its perfect bun so it rests on her shoulders.

"I think so," I say. "I mean, there are quite a few left. This was, what, the second one of the semester?"

She nods. "Well, I was thinking we could work

on our duo at tournaments. Get it written so we can have it polished before the season starts back up in January."

I didn't forget about our duo piece, exactly, but I'd sort of given up on it on the assumption that Billie had been avoiding me since the dragon incident. "That sounds fun. It would definitely help with all the downtime." This weekend alone, I spent at least fifteen hours just sitting around waiting for rounds to finish, which is standard for those of us who only compete in interp events.

Shocking me, Billie sets her trophy on her seat and hops across the aisle to join me in my own. Her thigh presses against mine, my skin burning even though we aren't technically touching. God, I'm in trouble with this girl.

She pulls up the Kindle app on her phone and scrolls through books while talking. "I was thinking about these books..." The list includes a few that we bought at the store a couple weeks ago, and a few that I've never heard of. We go over them for a while, although it's hard to focus with her arm brushing up against mine.

"You know," I say, suddenly shy. "You're like, really good. At acting. Are you going to school for it?"

She looks away, and is that a blush on her cheeks? It's hard to tell in the dim glow of her phone's light.

"No," she says with a short laugh. "I'm gonna be a mechanic. There's a community college pretty close."

One corner of my lips tilts down. "Oh." I chew my bottom lip and look out the window for a moment, building up my courage. "You should apply anyway. Just in case."

She shrugs, and now she's definitely avoiding my gaze.

I can't let this go, though. I know good acting when I see it. I've been surrounded by aspiring actors and retired actors and Broadway stars throughout my life. Maybe she can't see it, but I can.

"It's too expensive," she mumbles after a long awkward silence while I'm still trying to think of what to say. I brighten up immediately.

"Well, there are scholarships. NYU has a bunch for actors if you talk to the professors and your auditions go well."

She turns back to me, a flicker of hope shining in her eyes, but she's still guarded. How can I get through to her?

"Maybe," I say, carefully this time, "we could be roommates. That's where I plan to go after graduation."

A sad smile crosses her face. "Maybe."

God, she is frustrating. Can't she see how absolutely incredible she is? I don't want to push her too much, though. Her avoidance the past week has been agony, and I'm not sure I can go back to that.

"Well, just apply. No harm in applying," I say with a shrug. Then, I change the subject back to our spring duo, scrolling through Amazon on my phone to see if there are other pieces we may enjoy. Whatever we do, it has to be perfect.

It will be perfect.

When the bus pulls into the school's lot, Billie's head is resting on my shoulder, her hair tickling my throat. I smile, and she blushes when she sits up.

"See you on Monday," she says as we leave.

"I look forward to it."

Chapter Eleven
Theo

THE NEXT WEEKEND, I TEXT BILLIE through the whole tournament. Since the play is only a week away, preparation has taken over our afternoons, including Interp class. Combined with the fact that everyone and their brother wants to talk to Billie about the dragon attack, it means I've hardly gotten a word in with her. I'm lucky today that she even texts me back.

Maximus has taken a liking to shredding paper, which has made doing homework into a sporting event. Two days ago, I just decided to buy a ream of paper from Dollar General so that he would stop destroying my work.

The next text I receive stops me dead in my tracks, my hand hovering over the keyboard as I'm unable to respond.

Cool if I come over to work on Interp? Gonna be back in like half an hour.

A pleased flush moves through me, and I stare at my phone with the biggest grin on my face. Then, I take a look at my room and find that it's a conglomeration of shredded papers, fast food cups, and piles of laundry.

I have half an hour. First thing's first, I give Maximus to Nana, who's in bed with her reading glasses that take up half her face and a steamy romance novel.

"Girlfriend coming over?" she asks, stroking Max's head as he snuggles up to her neck.

My face goes hot. "She's not my girlfriend," I mumble.

I don't include that I might like for her to be. I'm sure Nana will be able to deduce that as soon as Billie walks in the door anyway.

I abandon Nana in her room and go back to

mine, gathering up all the shredded paper and assorted trash first. The moment my laundry goes into the washer downstairs, there's a knock at the door.

My heart races, and I rush to answer it. When I swing the door open, Billie is standing on my front porch in a pair of leggings and a maroon sweatshirt, her hair practically floating around her face. She must have had time to change before leaving the tournament today. An SUV drives off, a man in the driver's seat that must be her dad.

"How are you?" I ask, my cheeks warm once again. Billie is going to be in my house.

"Freezing," she says with a laugh. I bluster and invite her in, offering her a drink. We each get a glass of chocolate milk before going up to my room. I rush so she doesn't have to meet Mom, who will surely ask dozens of embarrassing questions.

We settle into a routine quickly, her reading lines from the book we've chosen and me typing them down. It's been so long since I've had friends over — not since I've lived in New York — that it's hard for me to grasp that she's actually here to spend time with me.

No, she just wants to work on our performance.

It's hard to think that when she gives me that blinding smile, though.

Chapter Twelve
Billie

THEO'S ROOM ISN'T WHAT I EXPECTED. With her constant fitness attire and generally stoic personality, I expected something dark and dreary, or perhaps some WWE posters. Instead, I'm sitting on an ornate vintage chair with gold detailing and pink floral fabric, and her bed has a set in nearly the same pattern. There's even a plush white faux fur rug on the ground, and I squish my bare toes over the soft fabric.

I dictate another line from the book, and the keys on Theo's laptop click softly under her hands, hands I want to hold.

I flush for what must be the thousandth time tonight, but she doesn't seem to notice, as she's too busy focusing on the computer screen. That's probably a good thing. She doesn't need to know just how hard I'm crushing on her. There's no reason to make this weird.

"Ugh," she says after I read the next line.

I look up, and she's closing her laptop and stretching. Her t-shirt lifts just a little above the hem of her leggings, and I catch a glimpse of her toned stomach beneath.

I look away.

"I think it's time for a snack break," she says, setting her laptop to the side. "I think my brain is melting. Why does cutting a piece have to be so boring?"

I don't mention that I actually enjoy the process of cutting a performance, shaving it here and there until it's an acceptable length for competitions. It's a slow process, sure, but it's so rewarding to make a novel or a script ten minutes long whilst still keeping the essence of the story in tact.

"Right," I say instead.

I follow her downstairs and lean against the counter while she digs around the cabinet for snacks.

"So what is there to do for fun around here?" she asks whilst half buried in a cupboard.

I shrug, then consider that she can't actually see me. "Not a lot. There's a lake pretty close but that's only fun in summer. Otherwise people tend to go to Knoxville over the weekend. And some people have barn parties, I guess." I don't include that I've never actually been invited to one of these parties. In fact, the only high school parties I've ever been to have been drama club cast parties. I'm not exactly socialite of the century.

"That makes sense," she says. Something in the cabinet crinkles, and Theo reappears with a sleeve of chocolate chip cookies. The super chewy kind.

My favorite.

She hands me one, and I lean against the counter and take a small bite out of it. No need to be rude and eat it all in one bite like I like doing. A moment later, though, Theo does just that. I smile.

A sound turns my head, a garbled squeak that

I can't quite place. I whip my head around, and a red ball is diving down the stairs, gliding clumsily on leathery wings.

My mouth goes dry, and my jaw drops. It can't be.

But it is.

The dragon chirps again, and when it reaches the bottom of the stairs, it skitters over before climbing up Theo like she's a perch. Theo's grandmother, who I recognize from the bookstore, trots down the stairs.

"Sorry," she says in a huff. "He was scratching at the door and ruining the paint."

"What the fuck?" I say, my voice the barest of whispers, but it's enough for Theo's eyes to lock on mine. I take a step back when the creature turns to me as well, its slitted gold eyes calculating. It's no bigger than a puppy, but I've seen just the type of danger it will pose when it's older. Fire flashes behind my eyes, and my throat closes up.

"Billie," Theo pleads, reaching an arm out. I jolt backwards, and the dragon does nothing but tilt its head at me.

I try to speak, to demand an explanation, but the words won't come out. It's like my voice has been stolen away. I back until I hit the rear door of the house, and I fumble for the handle. Theo looks hurt, her eyebrows tilting up with concern.

"Let me explain," she says, but I'm already out the door. I slam it behind me, and, once I know I'm safe, I run.

Chapter Thirteen
Billie

NOBODY IS HOME WHEN I FINALLY AR-
rive, and I collapse into my bed in my sweaty
clothes and fall fast asleep, my dreams filled with
fire and death.

The official count had been fifty-six. Fifty-six
lives lost when the dragon attacked the town.
One had been a girl my age, Tabitha. She'd been a
sweet and quiet girl, one who never caused drama
or complained. She'd been home alone when her
house collapsed on top of her. I see her, although
I don't know how I know it's her, as she's nearly eighteen in the dream. Her eyes hold the same

kindness, though. Until the dragon — I'm not sure if it's the one from five years ago or the one from the parade — rips her in half like she's made of paper.

I awaken in a cold sweat as thunder claps, shaking the house. I cover myself with my blanket, a shiver taking over my body. It doesn't stop.

The sun hasn't come out yet, but I climb out of bed, listening for signs that the thunder is more than that. I sneak across the house, the clock on the microwave showing that it's three in the morning, and I walk right into Dad's room.

After the dragon attack and the divorce, I would sleep in Dad's room, curled in a ball while my whole world fell apart around me. Tonight, I climb into his bed once again.

He stirs, reaching for the lamp on his side table.

"What's up, kiddo?" he asks, his voice gruff with sleep. He's in his usual nighttime getup, a white t-shirt and flannel pajama pants. His tattoos wind around his arms, one featuring wolves that run in never-ending strides. Only a few of his tattoos move, although the stationary ones remaining are still stunning. Dad doesn't have much for himself, but he has his tattoos.

"Can I sleep in here?" I ask, my voice embarrassingly small. Another rumble of thunder breaks across the sky, and I shiver again.

He doesn't hesitate to scoot over, and I bury myself under his comforter, keeping mine around me as an extra shield.

"Do you wanna talk about it?" he asks, concern seeping through every inch of his voice.

"Bad dreams," I say. I've always been able to talk to him about anything. "Tabitha. Dragons. The usual."

He sighs. "I'm sorry. Do you need me to stay home from work tomorrow? We can do a movie day." I tear up. How can one parent be so great whilst the other is the polar opposite?

I shake my head. "It's okay. I just didn't want to be alone."

He turns the light back off, but the door opens once again. Doris crawls in on Dad's other side without a word, and Einstein hops up after, letting out a satisfied sigh.

WHEN I WAKE IN THE MORNING, I'M alone in Dad's bed. My phone says it's nearly eleven in the morning, and the rain has stopped pattering against the windows, although the light is dim. Instead of getting up, I scroll through my notifications. I delete all twenty messages from Theo without reading them.

When I get to my email, one from my tech school stands out. Congratulations! is the subject line, so I click it and read through. The last sentence makes me do a double-take.

As we are not an accredited school, we were unable to process your FAFSA application. Please contact the bursar's office to arrange for payment totaling $3,125 for the fall of 2020.

They can't take my financial aid.

I can't...

The thought doesn't even complete itself. It's not possible. This was the plan. I was going to get my diesel tech certification, get a good job, and stay close to home. It was going to be fine.

Three thousand dollars is impossible. It's hardly even a real number. My paychecks and tips from the diner are just enough to keep my phone bill paid and the lights on. We can't spare anything else.

"What's wrong?" Doris asks, and I look up to find her standing in the doorway, her eyes wide. She's wearing that flat cap again, her hair tucked beneath. She's clearly going through her own thing, but I can't bring myself to ask what it is.

I touch my face to find that my cheeks are soaked with tears. Fuck. I'm supposed to stay strong for my sister, even if she is a little shit sometimes. I could lie, tell her that I was just reading a sad book about a dog. Instead, I say, "I can't go to college." My voice is hoarse, and it breaks on the last word. "It's too expensive." My hands shake and I drop my phone.

Doris doesn't make fun of me, doesn't come back with a snarky comment. Instead, she turns and leaves. Before I can question it, she returns, Einstein hot on her heels. She heaves him onto the bed, and he is comically large in her scrawny arms. When he sees me, he pads over and licks my face, and I half laugh, half sob.

"I'll be back in a few minutes," Doris says, and I pet Einstein until he lies on his chest. His weight is reassuring, like he's squeezing the anxiety right out of me. When Doris comes back yet again, she has a plate of brownies and a glass of chocolate milk. She clambers into bed with me and turns on the TV, switching it so we can watch Brooklyn Nine-Nine, starting with the episode where Rosa has to catch a guy dealing illegal potions.

"Thanks," I say, wrapping my sister in a hug. She squirms and groans, but I hold her tight. "You know, you aren't totally evil. I think there's a chance you're not the spawn of Satan."

She gasps, putting her hand on her chest when I finally release her. "You take that back. I am the Prince of Darkness."

The word choice gives me pause, but I roll my eyes. "Fine. But you're only, like, half demon. The other half might be an actual human being."

She sticks out her tongue and turns back to the

show.

By the time afternoon rolls around, my sadness has turned to righteous anger. If the cheap tech school is out of reach, I might as well shoot for the stars. With less hesitation than I expected, I finish the NYU application that I started on my phone and hit Submit.

Chapter Fourteen
Theo

ITRY TO CATCH BILLIE IN INTERP, BUT SHE completely avoids me, ignoring every word I speak to her. Kaylee gives me a look of pity, but she doesn't speak to me, either. I knew people in this town had a thing about dragons, but I didn't realize it could be serious enough that Billie would completely shut me out over it.

If she's not willing to talk to me, though, then I'm not going to keep trying. There's no point pining after someone who's just not interested. I double down on backstage prep for the play, and I don't speak a word to Billie, silently passing her props as needed.

It's fine. Everything is fine.

I try to search for dragon rescue groups in the area, but it's hard to find anywhere here that takes care of mountain dragons, as they usually live hundreds of miles further North, merely passing through the central Appalachians to get further South for the winter. The nearest wild dragon rescue is five hours away.

When rehearsal is over, I put all the props back in their proper spots, double checking that everything is where it belongs. I'm walking home today, as Nana only lives a mile away, but Kaylee catches me on my way out the door.

"Hey, what's going on with you and Billie," she asks, her hand tight around my arm so I can't escape.

So Billie hasn't told anybody. Odd.

I shrug. Time to lie. "I told her that I like her, and I guess she doesn't feel the same way."

Kaylee's mouth turns into a half-frown. "Hm," she says. There's a pause while she considers my words, and I almost think she's gonna call me out on the lie. Instead, she says, "I don't know why she'd say that. She's obviously into you."

I try to keep my face straight and just shrug again. When she lets me go, I say goodbye and walk home, but I can't stop thinking about what she said. Is Billie into me? Wouldn't I be able to tell? By the time I walk through the front door, I decide that Kaylee is delusional.

The play is next weekend, so I should just focus on that.

Chapter Fifteen
Billie

"BILLIE!" THE WORST VOICE IN THE WORLD calls as I'm walking to my History of Witch-craft class. I sigh and turn to find Tom following me and waving a piece of paper.

"What do you want?" I ask in the most mono-tone voice I can muster. He will not leave me alone, constantly trying to convince me that he would've killed the dragon if I hadn't taken his sword, or that I'm some type of modern hero. Whatever.

He puts an arm over my shoulders jovially, ig-noring me when I shrug it off. When he tries to put a hand on my arm, I slap it away and his eyes tighten just a little. "I was hoping you'd sign my petition. We're trying to get a state clearance to exterminate the rest of the flock of mountain dragons. They haven't left Bore's Grove for some reason."

My mind flashes to the baby dragon that had treated Theo like its parent, its wide golden eyes and infantile squeaking. Are they staying for that creature? "No, thanks," I say, continuing on to my class.

"Oh, come on, Billie," he says. "You hate the dragons more than anybody." The whine in his voice is just like the one Doris uses when she's being particularly bratty, like this morning when Dad wouldn't drive her to the middle school that's three blocks from the house. I grind my teeth.

I shrug. "I don't hate them. I just don't want to be around them."

He spins me around by my upper arm, and I slap his hand once again.

"Seriously, Tom. Don't touch me," I say, teeth gritted.

He rolls his eyes. "C'mon, Billie. We all know they'd be better off gone. They've killed people."

I sigh. I hate Tom, but I can't deny that he has a point. Still, I don't think it would be right to kill the dragons. They're not monsters, just wild animals doing what they need to survive. The two dragons that have been in Bore's Grove had been outliers. "I'll think about it. Now let me go to class."

He grins, his eyes shining with excitement. "Thanks, Dragon Slayer."

As he's running away to get to his own class, I call back, "Don't call me that!"

It won't help, of course. Everyone has been calling me that lately.

Maybe I should have a conversation with Theo. The thought makes my heart race and my throat close up, though.

Maybe tomorrow.

Chapter Sixteen
Theo

IN INTERP AND PLAY REHEARSAL FRIDAY afternoon, I catch Billie looking at me. Still, though, she hasn't spoken to me, although it's been nearly a week since the incident at my house. Every time I notice her, she looks away.

Okay, this is getting ridiculous. I need to ask her why she didn't spill my secret to anyone, and I almost want to ask why Kaylee thinks she likes me. I shake that thought away, and, when play rehearsal ends, I set out and hike the three miles to the off-interstate diner where half the theatre troupe works.

When I get inside, I'm shivering from the late

autumn air. Halloween decorations dot the diner, glowing in the dim light since the sun has already cascaded past the mountains, plunging our valley into darkness. A vampire woman is sitting at the counter and cutting into a rare — okay, raw — steak, and a truck driver with fox ears and a tail is sitting at his own booth. Other than that, I'm alone in the diner.

A siren girl with bluish-black hair saunters up to the hostess stand, blasting a million-watt smile at me. I blink in surprise, and she asks, her voice husky, "Booth or table?"

I gulp. "I was hoping that you could put me in Billie's section. We're friends from school?" The last sentence is upturned like I'm not sure of myself, and my words come out dry and hoarse.

"Of course," she says, casting her eyes down and then back at me. Is she flirting?

She leads me to a table and sets a menu down.

"We're having a special on cherry pie," she says with a wink, and I flush and look away. Is there something in the water here making every girl in town gorgeous or something?

"Thanks," I mumble and put the menu in front of my face to hide my embarrassment. I've only met a few sirens, and every single one of them has had that effect on me. Not everyone is affected by sirens, but when they are, said reaction is pretty extreme.

A moment later, Billie comes to the table, her eyes on something else as she says, "Welcome to Gordon's, can I get you..." She trails off when her eyes meet mine.

"Hey," I say shyly.

She bites her bottom lip, and I dart my eyes to her lips for just an instant before meeting her eyes once again.

"I was thinking we should talk," I say. "Just for a few minutes."

She looks to the service station, where the hostess, Kaylee, and two other servers are leaning against the counter chatting, then at the door, which yields zero new customers. She could retreat to the kitchen, but she doesn't. She just stands there.

"I just wanted to know..." I hesitate. I should

definitely not ask her about what Kaylee said earlier in the week. That would be weird. Really weird. "Why you didn't tell anyone about Maximus." After a brief pause, I clarify, "The dragon."

She taps her fingers against her notepad, looking at the door once again, but nobody has arrived.

"I didn't think it was my place," she says. "But I don't think we should have this conversation here."

I'm about to protest, but she cuts me off. "I'm off at nine. Can I come over to talk then?"

I swallow. Billie is coming to my house again?

"Sure," I find myself saying.

This is just to talk about Maximus, I remind myself, but it doesn't matter. My heart is racing, and I'm still dwelling on the conversation I had with Kaylee.

I order something to-go, waving briefly as I step out into the chilly night air. It's quite a walk home, and I have to make sure I'm ready.

Chapter Seventeen
Billie

FILICIA DROPS ME OFF AT THE VICTORI-
an house on the hill after our shifts end. She
doesn't ask what I'm doing here, just raises her
eyebrows at me one last time when I climb out of
the car.

"We're just going to talk about our duo for this
spring," I lie for what must be the fifth time.

"Uh-huh." She pulls away. I guess I'll have to
walk home. I text Dad that I'm hanging out with
a friend for a bit before coming home, then slip
my phone into the pocket of my uniform black
slacks that I hate. I wrap my dark red leather jacket

around myself to keep out the biting wind before approaching the front door.

A moment after I knock, a middle-aged woman answers, her dark hair in an elegant updo that I could never pull off. She's smiling down at me, as she's even taller than Theo. "You must be Billie. Lovely to finally meet you." She lets me in, and Theo comes thundering down the stairs.

"You can come on up," she says, her eyes lingering on the woman for a second too long. "Mom, please don't harass my friend."

The word "friend" seems like a stretch, but I don't know how much her family knows. "Nice to meet you," I mumble to her mom before following Theo upstairs.

Before Theo opens the door to her bedroom, she evaluates me. "Maximus is in here," she says, her voice careful. "He's in the cage I built him, but I didn't want you to be startled."

I set my jaw and nod once. "I'll be fine." I'm not sure whether it's a lie or not.

Theo sets her hand on the doorknob, tiny electric sparks flying into the handle when she turns it. Is she an astrapomancer? I don't ask, as I'm immediately focused on the dragon bouncing around within the glowing ball of magical energy tucked into the corner of her room.

I take in a deep breath, hold it for a five second count, then release it before taking a step into the room. I stay close to the door, and Theo has to squeeze past me to sit on her bed. She watches me, gauging my reaction.

I try to make light conversation. "Why Maximus?"

She looks to him, then back to me. "Nana named him. She's really into animated movies."

"Ah."

I take the slowest step in the world, then another. Within a few strides, I'm close enough to the ceiling-height enclosure to touch it.

"It's not dangerous," Theo says. "It's just a basic barrier so he can't get out."

I nod, but I don't reach out.

"Why do you have him?" Maximus chirps at me, climbing up the wall deftly to look me in the eyes. He looks just like the one I killed.

"He fell in our pool and almost died. I'm trying to find a rescue organization, but there's nothing in this area."

"When?" I ask, lifting my fingers just enough for Maximus to notice. He's almost cute, but I can't help but wonder how many people he'll try to kill when he gets older.

She confirms my suspicions. "The night of the parade."

I sigh. "So the one I...the one that landed. Do you think that could be why?"

Theo doesn't respond, and I look at her. She's sitting straight as a board and staring at the floor. What did I say?

"I think," she says slowly, "it may have been his mother."

My heart crashes. If Theo is right, then I'd killed a mother that was just trying to find her baby. "You almost died," I whisper. "She was going to kill you."

Theo stands up and walks to me, but she keeps a respectable distance. "I know," she says. "I don't think you could've done anything different. And

I'm grateful, I really am. But…" She turns to look at Maximus, and so do I.

"But now he's an orphan," I finish for her. I walk over to the vintage chair and collapse, tossing an arm across my eyes. I try to recall Tom's words in the hallway earlier this week. "The rest of the flock is still here, though. I think they might be looking for him. But people in town think they should just exterminate the rest of them."

Theo's bed squeaks with weight, but I don't uncover my eyes.

"Is that what you want?" she asks.

I don't answer right away, considering her words carefully. It's true that mountain dragons terrify me, but do the actions of one determine the fate of the rest?

"No," I say, and an invisible weight lifts off my shoulders.

"Then I think we should return Maximus to the flock," Theo says.

"What are you talking about?" I ask, jerking my arm away. Theo isn't looking at me, though. Her eyes follow Maximus as he plays with a rock at the bottom of his homemade barrier.

"If we return him, then maybe they'll leave. The town can't kill them if they're not here, right?"

She's making a lot of sense, but…

"How are we supposed to find a flock of mountain dragons? And not die?" I ask. Being in the room with a baby is hard enough for me to bear. Running into a whole flock of dragons bigger than my house? No way.

She doesn't argue, just sits in contemplation for a few moments. "You don't have to help," she says. Her tone is distant, like she's already busy thinking of something else.

I groan. "Fine. Fine. I will help. But if I so much as think that I hear an adult dragon, I'm out. And we have to wait until after the play next weekend. I'm the lead, and I can't die before opening night."

"Deal," Theo says.

Chapter Eighteen
Billie

THE DAYS BEFORE WE OPEN ARE ABSO-
lute murder. Nielsen has us in rehearsal until
nine every night, and we're running the play twice
a day with an hour of notes. I hardly get a moment
to speak to Theo, and all she can talk about is finding the dragons. She has a bunch of apps on her
phone, and she's joined a few forums that track
that sort of thing.

"MaxDragons10?" I ask, snorting at her pen
name.

She sticks her tongue at me. "You try better."

I shrug and go back to working through my first

scene with Tom after Nielsen is finished putting him through the ringer during Interp. He keeps screwing up one part, which is starting to get on my. nerves. Combined with him badgering me every day about his disgusting petition, and I just want the play to be over.

On the drive home, Kaylee and Filicia keep giving each other looks.

"Oh my god, what?" I ask, leaning forward from the backseat.

Kaylee glances at me in the rearview mirror.

"I think you know what," she says meaningfully.

"Billie and Theo, sitting in a tree, K-I-S-S—" Filicia sings, laughing maniacally when I slap her lightly on the arm.

"We're just friends," I mumble.

"Uh-huh," Kaylee says, but even that simple sound is filled with skepticism.

Filicia turns to me. "That's not what I heard."

I blush. "What are you talking about?"

"Ugh," Kaylee says. "You're the worst liar. Theo told me what she said to you. I can't believe you rejected her."

Wait, what?

"I, uh —" I stammer, but there are no words for what they just said. It doesn't make sense. Why does nothing surrounding Theo make sense?

"I mean, everyone knows you're into her," Kaylee says. "So I don't see why you'd lie to her when she finally confesses her feelings.

I can't speak. My voice is well and truly gone. What is she talking about?

Thankfully, she pulls into my driveway, and I leap out of the car into the cold darkness. Einstein is barking at the door, and I run in, calling, "See you tomorrow!" Maybe I won't look like a total weirdo if I'm at least mildly polite.

I press my back against the front door and let out a sigh.

Dad and Doris are sitting on the couch, sharing a bowl of popcorn and watching the credits roll on what could only be a Marvel movie.

"How was rehearsal?" Dad asks.

I consider giving him any details but I just can't, especially not in front of Doris. "I'm going to bed.

Early morning."

Chapter Nineteen
Billie

"ARE YOU COMING TO THE CAST PARTY at Tom's house?" I ask as Theo buttons me into my first gown of the night. We've still got an hour to curtain, but there are twenty people in the cast who also have to get ready, and Nielsen has to do everyone's makeup herself.

It's the second and final night of the play—that's all we have the budget for—and everything has run smoothly so far. Tom is finally hitting the notes in his songs, and Kaylee and Filicia have stopped harassing me about Theo's crush, which I've determined she must have made up. Heat rushes over my shoulders as Theo's fingers lithely trace over my back with the buttons.

"I don't know," she says. "I'm not really part of the group."

I laugh. "Of course you are." I see where she's coming from, though. She hasn't been here that long, and she doesn't seem to talk to a lot of people except the occasional conversation with Kaylee. Maybe she's closer with people in her other classes?

"Would there even be space for me?"

"Tom can make space," I say. He's currently sitting on a stool getting his makeup applied. "Everyone is invited to the cast parties, and it's a good time." I can practically hear Theo coming up with more arguments as to why she should attend, so I continue, "I think it would be really fun if you came." I'm glad she's behind me and that I'm covered in thick stage makeup, because I must be red as a lobster right now. I can't stop thinking about what Kaylee said, even if it had been a cover.

"There, all buttoned," she says. I turn to face her, tilting my head back because she's standing so close. She doesn't take a step back, and neither do I. "The party sounds fun. I guess I could come for an hour or so."

I grin and wrap my arms around her neck, and she stumbles back.

I pull away. "Sorry. Got too excited." Yeah, now I'm definitely red. But I almost think that she might be, too.

When the curtain goes up, she pats me once on the shoulder, and that space burns through the rest of the play.

Chapter Twenty
Billie

I'M PLEASANTLY SURPRISED WHEN THEO descends the stairs into Tom's basement. She's still wearing her Theatre Blacks, the all-black apparel that stage crew must wear throughout the play. Her hair is no longer hidden under a black cap, though, instead flowing over her shoulders in loose curls.

I give a little wave, and I don't miss the significant look Kaylee gives me from over by the arcade games.

Theo moves over to me, and I scoot over on the

couch, leaning to the cooler to grab her a soda.

"Thanks," she says, her voice raised over the music.

Tonight, I'm going to ask her if what Kaylee said is true. If she's actually interested in me. I have to know. Even though I dismissed it earlier in the week, I still can't stop thinking about it.

"What do you want to do first? There's pinball, a shooting game, a pool table, foosball…" I list off. Tom's dad is pretty much the only lawyer in town, so they have a huge house with an amazing basement. They also only live two blocks from Theo's house.

"Foosball," Theo says, standing up and offering her hand. I smile and take it. Her skin is so soft. "I should warn you, I'm basically a pro." I laugh and follow her over. When we approach the table, two freshmen are just arriving as well.

"Teams?" I offer as they're about to walk away upon seeing us.

As it turns out, I am terrible at foosball. And if Theo were a pro, she would've been dropped from the team. We only score a single point against the other team despite our best efforts, although I blame the distraction of our shoulders and hands touching almost constantly.

We also try out the ancient shooting game, which gives us the choice of a red and a blue gun. I pick blue, and Theo takes red. We get shot by too many aliens to count, but at least it's fun. I laugh at Theo's dismal score, and she points out that mine isn't much better.

"I need some quiet," she practically shouts over the now booming pop karaoke music.

"I'm gonna take my horse..." Filicia and Tom yell-sing into the game's microphone. I cringe. They're both trained singers, for goodness' sake.

I trot up the steps after Theo, who takes them two at a time. The dull thrum of bass is still shaking in my feet, but it's more bearable up here.

Nobody from theatre is upstairs anymore, and I grab a water bottle from the counter. An older boy gets up from the kitchen table and walks out the door, keys jingling as he goes.

"Who was that?" Theo asks, lifting an eyebrow. "He didn't even say hi."

I nod. "Tom's brother, Kayden. He goes to school in Nashville, but I guess he's in town for the weekend."

"That's quite a drive," she replies, taking a sip out of her unfinished soda.

"He's always coming around. He's some sort of town hero because he and his friends were the ones who saw the dragon coming into town. They got a bunch of people to start evacuating before it attacked."

Theo frowns. "How did they see it?"

I shrug. "I guess they were out hiking or something."

She goes still, her expression contemplative. What is she thinking about? Her eyes find a laptop sitting open on the table where he'd been sitting.

"Do you remember what we said last weekend?"

All I can think about is the fact that Theo apparently told Kaylee that she likes me.

"No," I say honestly.

"About how the dragon that landed at the parade probably did so because of Maximus?"

I nod. "Right. Yeah."

"Well, I looked up mountain dragon behavior, and they tend to avoid humans. Overall, they're really shy." She walks over to the table and sits in front of the laptop. Before I can say anything, she's using the trackpad and opening random folders.

"Theo," I hiss, but she ignores me.

"What if the dragon that wrecked town had a reason?" Theo asks. "And what if Kayden knows what that reason is? If he was one of the first ones to see the dragon…"

"Theo, his best friend died in the attack." It doesn't exactly negate her point, but I can't think of anything else to do to get her to stop this breach of privacy. "We should really go," I press, but then a video pops up on the screen.

A voice is speaking, a male voice. It sounds like Tom, but a little more nasally. Perhaps a younger Kayden? It says, "You guys, shut up. We can't get caught."

There's a flashlight beam, and the sound of footsteps on stone. The rush of water. Wind battering the microphone.

Another masculine voice, this one further from the camera, laughs, and a third tells him to be quiet. "Seriously," Kayden — I assume — says.

"What is this?" I ask, leaning forward and squinting. The video is nearly black, and any details are impossible to make out.

Another noise bursts in, a quick squawk that I recognize instantly. A baby dragon. The camera darts forward and takes a moment to focus as multiple flashlights point at the nest of animal bones and rocks and dead grass. A baby mountain dragon, quite a bit larger than Maximus but still clearly young, has its head raised, eyes flashing gold in the beams of light.

Illness begins to well in my stomach, and bile rises in my throat even though nothing has technically happened in the video.

"Quick, quick," the laughing boy says with a grin. He appears on camera, wearing an all-black stealth outfit like I've only ever seen in military movies and games. His face is uncovered, and I recognize his shoulder-length, unkempt hair and glass-cut features instantly. It's not hard to recognize Mike Trotter, the boy whose death was publicized as the greatest tragedy of the entire town's destruction. He was the pride of the town, the star football player who signed up to join the marines and serve the nation. I never knew him, as I was only thirteen when he died, but I knew of him. Including the anonymous posts on Tumblr that talked about his dad covering up an alleged sexual assault that Mike had been involved in.

In the video, he pulls a huge bowie knife out of a sheath strapped to his thigh, and the dragon sniffs the air toward him and squawks again. I rest my hand on Theo's shoulder, and she intertwines her fingers with mine.

When Mike slits the dragon's throat, Kayden and the other boy laugh. They laugh. Theo squeezes my hand, and tears stream down her face.

But the video isn't over. The boys laugh and rush out of what is clearly a cave, hopping into a red pickup truck. A grin is splayed across Mike's face, along with streaks of red like some sort of fucked up war paint. Mike drives, and the camera flashes over another boy, clearly younger than the rest. Brent's face is a little chubbier than now, but I know him because he lives in the same trailer park as me. He's grinning just as wildly as Mike, and then when Kayden turns the camera on himself, I'm not even surprised.

A rumble shakes them, and Mike laughs out loud. "Come and get me, bitch!" he shouts, leaning his head out the window. The camera shakes and jolts until it's facing the sky, where an adult mountain dragon dives toward the cave they just left. I've seen that dragon before, once in real life and a thousand times in my nightmares.

I hit the spacebar before the video can go on. I remember what happens next well enough. The dragon will chase the red pickup into town, blasting fire as it goes. Destroying everyone.

"Holy shit," Theo says, her voice breaking. After a brief pause, she grabs the cable hanging off the computer and plugs it in to her phone, dragging the file over to make a copy. "Everyone has to see this."

"Wait, what?" I say, attempting to shake away the fear gripping me tight. It doesn't work.

"They want to kill the dragons," she says. "People have to know the truth."

"But can't Kayden, like, sue or something?" I don't even know if it's true, but I have to channel my fear into something.

"I don't care," she says, unplugging her phone and standing.

I really shouldn't argue. She's not wrong. I think I'm in shock. When she goes to the door and wrenches it open, I'm still staring at the laptop, which is back to the plain home screen.

"Are you coming?" she asks, her voice short.

I look at her slowly. "Yeah," I find myself saying.

It only takes a few minutes to walk to her house, and we go straight to her room. Nobody intercepts us on our way up.

Maximus isn't in the corner, and the magical shield is gone.

"Nana must have him," Theo mumbles, loading up the video on her phone. I don't watch it this time, and she doesn't pause it like I did. As it turns out, Kayden never stopped recording. The video is long, ridiculously long. Mercifully, she does hit mute at the part where Mike dies. I can't possibly listen to his screams.

When the video is over, I collapse to the floor.

"What are we gonna do?" I ask.

Tears blur my vision, falling down into the soft faux fur rug. I don't know how I can do this. My whole life is falling apart around me. It's like I don't know anything anymore.

"We have to go to the police," Theo says, resolved. I'm glad she's strong, because there's no possible way I can be. "They'll know what to do."

After a pause, movement comes from Theo's direction, and she sits on the floor next to me, putting her hand over mine. A comforting gesture only, I'm sure.

"Everything is going to be alright."

Chapter Twenty-One
Theo

BILLIE STAYS THE NIGHT AT MY HOUSE. Billie. In my house. She sleeps on the couch downstairs after letting her dad know that she won't be home, and it takes me hours to fall asleep, her presence unbearable below me. I imagine reaching down to her with my mind, thoughts intertwining.

I wake up early, the light streaming in golden. Last night takes a moment to reload in my mind, and I jolt up, jogging downstairs in my pajamas. The wooden floors are absolutely frigid, but I ignore the cold.

"Billie?" I say, and she stirs, turning over on the couch. She's still wearing her clothes from yesterday, but there's no time for us to go elsewhere so she can get cleaned up.

"Time to go?" she asks groggily.

I nod. "Yeah. Let's end this."

The walk to the police station doesn't take long. It's just down the hill at the square, and I hold the door open for Billie, who's at least managed to put her hair up and wash her face. I clutch a flash drive in my hand, something solid I can give to the officer in charge rather than just showing him the video on my phone.

When we approach the counter, though, I'm at a loss for words.

"Can we speak with Chief Trotter?" Billie asks before I have the chance to reconsider my life choices.

"Do you have an appointment?" the young man in uniform sitting at the counter asks.

"No," she says, suddenly less sure of herself.

"But we were friends with Mike," I lie. Maybe it'll be enough to get us through the door.

The officer, not much older than us, turns from bored to sympathetic. "Of course," he says. "His office is right down the hall and to the left. He should be in there." After a pause, he awkwardly says, "Sorry for your loss."

Mike's death was five years ago, but I don't point that out. Instead, we thank him and continue to the chief's office on our own.

"That was shockingly easy," Billie mumbles.

When we reach his office, we find a middle-aged man with a slim build and a thick mustache on the phone, his eyebrows bunched together and his mouth an almost comical frown. When he looks up and sees us, though, he says something into the phone and hangs up.

"Can I help you ladies?" he asks, standing and stretching his hand out for us to shake. We do, although I don't appreciate the sweat now coating my hand. I wipe it on my leggings as subtly as possible.

"I hope so," I say. Confidence is key here. We just have to pretend we know what we're doing, and we'll get what we want. That's what Dad always says, and he's got a townhouse on Park Avenue. "We have a video from the dragon attack that we think might shine a light on the situation. We've heard about the petition to hunt down the mountain dragons, and we thought this might help save them."

"The attack from five years ago," Billie clarifies. I'm so glad she came with.

Chief Trotter's eyebrows squish together once again. "Aren't you the girl that killed this last one?"

Billie's face only reddens a little at that, and she straightens. "Yes, but that was due to the urgency of the situation."

He nods, but it seems like he's already tuning out. I hold up the flash drive, and he takes it.

"You might pause it after six minutes," Billie says before he double clicks the folder on his outdated desktop computer. "It gets graphic after that."

I don't mention that the most graphic part is where his son burns to death. As long as he pauses it, he won't have to learn that. Maybe I should've trimmed the video before copying it over. All the damning evidence is in that first six minutes, anyway.

He doesn't turn the sound on, but it's easy to tell what's going on in the video. His face is stoic, but something changes the moment Mike comes on screen. His jaw tightens just so, and so do his eyes. This must be hard on him, but there's not a lot we can do.

When he pauses it where I asked, he continues to watch the screen for a moment. Finally, after what feels like years, he turns to us.

"Is this the only copy of this video?" he asks. His voice is suddenly exhausted, like he's aged a hundred years since the moment we walked in.

"Yes," I lie. The look on his face unsettles me. There's something off about it, like he might hurt us.

This was a mistake.

"Thank you for bringing this in," he says. "I will make sure it gets in the right hands."

Liar.

"I don't think you should tell anybody else what you saw in this video. No need to alarm everyone in town with this."

I nod. "No problem. Just thought the authorities should see it."

After a polite goodbye, I walk out of the building, Billie trailing behind me.

When we make it down the block, she confirms my fear, "He's gonna destroy the evidence."

I nod. "This was a mistake. We aren't gonna get any help here."

Chapter Twenty-Two
Billie

THE FIRST THING I HEAR AT SCHOOL ON Monday morning is Tom's voice, and he's giving me the worst news. "They've approved the hunt!" he says, clapping me on the back, and I drop the book I'd been grabbing from my locker. "You should totally come. You could learn how you actually take out a dragon."

My stomach roils at his words. I grimace. "Leave me the fuck alone," I bite at him whilst picking up the book.

I don't have the energy to be polite to Tom. Not today.

He pulls back and frowns. "What got your panties in a twist? Did something happen at the party?" He's blocking me from leaving my locker, and my blood absolutely boils. How much trouble would I get in for punching him?

"No, Tom, it's just that you're the biggest asshole and always have been, and you think you're better than me for some reason. You can't sing on-key, and you can't stop pissing yourself long enough to actually save someone from a dragon. So just leave. Me. Alone."

His eyes are filled with hurt, but he's stunned enough that I can shove past him. Fuck him, and fuck everyone in this school. My eyes sting at the corners, and I rush into the bathroom and hide in the accessible stall in the corner before the tears come.

I hate this school, hate these people, hate that I had to be the one to kill the dragon. I wish I could just get away, go somewhere that nobody knows me. It would be easier that way.

With trembling hands, I open my phone to scroll through social media as a distraction. Instead, the red dot on my email app informs me that I have a new message. Probably spam.

When I open my inbox, though, it's an email from NYU Admissions.

Must be nothing, I think, but I open the email anyway.

Most of the words are a blur, but my eyes focus on the sentence, Please schedule your video audition.

Schedule an audition?

Wait.

Does that mean I have a chance? I'd just applied to their program on a whim with no real hope of getting in.

Before I can get too excited, I lock my phone and suck in a deep breath, pushing it out slowly.

The tears are gone, but my heart feels like it's going to implode.

The door to the restroom squeaks open, and Theo's voice reverberates through the room. "Billie? Are you okay?"

Shit. I use my phone's reverse camera as a mirror to make sure my makeup isn't ruined. I don't want people to know I've been crying, especially not Theo.

"Yeah," I say, but my voice squeaks.

I half expect her to leave, but of course she doesn't. Instead, her feet show up outside the stall door.

"Do you want to talk?" she asks.

I sigh. "I don't know," I say honestly.

Her weight shifts to one foot, and her bag shuffles with the change. The hall becomes quiet, and the first bell of the day rings. We're late for class. Still, neither of us moves.

"This sucks," she finally says. "Like, you can try absolutely everything to get people to listen, show them all the proof in the world, and they just won't."

I nod, then remember she can't actually see me in here. "Right," I say.

"And then, when you get mad they won't listen, they tell you that you're the one being hysterical, and maybe if you'd calm down, you'd be taken seriously. It's just...." She makes a frustrated sound.

I sigh. "Yeah."

I am so not in the mood to talk right now, but Theo's words ring true, and not just with the dragon situation. With everything. I open the stall door and walk past Theo to lean against the sink.

"Wanna ditch?" I ask. I have never once skipped class. Today, though, I have no patience for it, and it's not like I can get kicked out of play rehearsal because of it. The play is over.

It's only now that I'm here with Theo that the bathroom feels tiny. She towers over me, her blonde hair falling in a curtain around her. I imagine, for a moment, what it would be like for her to put her hands on either side of me and kiss me, but I shake it off.

"Sounds fun," she says, a wicked grin crossing her face.

I'm tense the whole way to her house, and I almost think I can hear a police siren. Are we going to get caught? Are there legal ramifications for skipping school without notifying your parents?

I have to speed walk to keep up with her, and I wrap my arms around myself to keep warm on the crisp autumn morning. Winter will be here soon, and this walk will be impossible. When we make it up the hill, we sneak in through the back door and tiptoe up to her room, although there aren't any cars in the driveway.

Theo collapses into her bed, and I curl up in the armchair, dropping my backpack on the floor in front of me.

"Maybe we should find the dragons," I say despite my instincts screaming that it's a terrible idea. "We can't do anything about the hunting permit, but we can try our best to get them out of here, right?"

Theo makes a sound of muffled affirmation, although she doesn't sit up.

I go to the magical cage, and Maximus lifts his head out from under his wing, his eyes droopy with sleep.

"Do you want to find them?" I ask, although there's no possible way he can understand me. I bite my lip and look at Theo. She's not going to take me seriously if I clearly can't stand to be around dragons. "Can I hold him?"

She sits up slowly and evaluates me. It makes

sense she would be skeptical. I'm skeptical, and it was my question.

When she waves the barrier away, I look back at Maximus. My throat closes up and my heart races, but I keep a straight face.

I reach a hand out, slower than should be possible, and he leans forward to sniff it. I resist jerking away at the hot breath against my sensitive fingertips.

"He doesn't bite," Theo clarifies.

I highly doubt that, as he's still a wild animal, but I don't take my eyes off him or reply to Theo. He stands and stretches, and I stay perfectly still, imagining that I'm completely invisible. When he puts a foot on my arm, a shiver runs through me, but I don't move. I stay as still as possible as he climbs up my arm, much like he did to Theo the first time I saw him. I gulp when he makes it up to my shoulder, his surprisingly smooth tail wrapping just around the curve of my neck and resting on my collarbone.

"He likes you," Theo says. I let out a short bark of a laugh, and Maximus chirps, causing me to flinch.

A moment later, though, he lies down and rests his head on my other collarbone, asleep in an instant.

"This isn't so bad," I admit, my voice tight. I turn back to Theo, and she's beaming. I can't say anything else when faced with her delight, so I just smile back at her.

Chapter Twenty-Three
Theo

WE CAN'T FIND THE DRAGONS. THEY don't seem to be anywhere. After leaving my house, Maximus curled up in bed with Nana, we try for the mountains. We borrow Nana's truck to cover as much ground as possible, but there's no sign of dragons anywhere near people have claimed they've been spotted.

We only skip the one day of class, but we go out every day after school to search for them, but they're just...gone. Still, we hear reports in town about people seeing them, plans for hunting them down. If nothing else, I don't think the hunting parties will be able to track them down.

Since Billie works on Thursday, I go out by myself. Unsurprisingly, I've come up with nothing as the sun sets over the mountains.

I take in a deep, shuddering breath after pulling into the driveway at home. My breath hitches, and tears prick at my eyes. Is Maximus going to be alone for the rest of his life? Will he ever see his family again?

I take out my phone and scroll through the contacts until I find the number I'm looking for, then hit "Call."

The longer it rings, the faster my heart races in my chest. Please answer, please answer, please -

"Hello, you've reached Steven Thompson. I'm not available to—" I hang up before the message finishes. A fat tear spills out of my eye and onto the steering wheel, and then another, and then another.

I can't do this.

A knock at the window startles me out of my stupor, and I find Nana watching me with concern in her eyes. Maximus is standing on her shoulder, head cocked at me. I unlock the truck, and she climbs into the passenger side, Maximus crawling into her lap before falling into a near instant sleep.

"What's going on?" Nana asks, stroking Maximus's wings.

I frown. "Nothing."

Nana rolls her eyes. "Ever since you and your mother moved here, you've been quiet and mopey. Spending time with Billie seems to help, but I know there's something wrong. You aren't the first teenage girl I've had in that house, you know."

"I know," I say, but it comes out too sharp. I turn so I'm looking out the window.

Nana doesn't reply. I expect her to chastise me for my tone, but she just sits there.

"I haven't talked to Dad since we came here," I admit when the silence becomes unbearable. "And when I finally tried to call him today, he didn't answer." The lump in my throat is getting bigger and bigger, and I gasp out a sob on the last word.

She still doesn't speak, so I continue, "And Mom doesn't care at all. She made me leave home, and I'm stuck here with no friends, and I don't get to go to my school, which I worked really hard to get into. And Maximus might never see his family again, and Billie doesn't think of me the same way I think of her, which is driving me up the freaking wall because I can't stop thinking about her."

Maybe I should be embarrassed at this outburst, but I'm just so tired of holding everything in. I don't have anybody to talk to about these things, and it's been building inside me until I finally exploded.

"First of all," Nana says, her voice kind and calm, a contrast to my desperate rambling, "your mother is doing her absolute best. She wonders every single day if she made the right decision coming here, but she had nothing left in New York. No job, no skills, no money.

"As for Maximus, he will be just fine. We can contact a rescue organization that will bring him in and take him to a zoo. I've heard St. Louis has a great dragon program, and he'd surely be perfectly happy there."

I nod, but I don't feel any better by her response. In fact, I only feel more guilty at how I've treated

Mom.

"Theodosia Thompson, you are the strongest young woman I've ever met in my life. You have done so much that kids your age couldn't even dream of, and I am more proud of you than I can explain. If your father can't see that, then he's a damn fool. And you may not see it, but it's clear that Billie thinks pretty highly of you."

I look at the ground. It can't be true.

However, I think back to how Billie has been acting around me. She was quick to welcome me onto the Interp squad, she saved my life, and she was quick to forgive me after finding out that her greatest fear was in my home. Hope blooms in my chest, tiny and delicate, but it's there.

"Do you really think so?" I ask, finally looking back at Nana.

"Absolutely," she says.

I nod. "Thanks, Nana."

Chapter Twenty-Four
Theo

FRIDAY IS A TEACHER'S WORK DAY, SO WE have the day off of school. Still, I wake up at seven in the morning, my phone's alarm blaring. I sit up and turn it off, glaring at my phone for a moment before putting it back under my pillow.

After a few minutes, though, I take it back out, waving the spell off so Maximus can join me on the bed. Nana is supposed to take him to a wildlife rescue organization in Knoxville later today, and they'll be transferring him to a zoo in North Carolina. I scroll through social media for a few minutes, but a post that Billie shared gives me pause. It's a totally innocuous post, an underexposed photo from the play last weekend. I can't help but trace the contours of her face with my eyes, and I sigh.

Before I can overthink it, I send her a text.

Can I come over?

BILLIE'S HOUSE IS ON THE OUTSKIRTS OF town, which isn't saying much since this town is so tiny. I park Nana's pickup next to an older model SUV, putting the keys in the pocket of my maroon leggings. I flex my hand, ready to ring the doorbell, when the dark gray door opens to reveal a girl who can't be more than thirteen.

"Billie, your friend is here," she calls, running off.

A man is sitting at the kitchen table. I recognize him from quick glances around town, but I've never actually met Billie's father. "Come on in," he says, and I open the plexiglass door. He stands and strides over to me, and I have to blink twice. He's tall, much like ninety percent of people in Bore's

Grove. He has soft blue eyes and a sprinkling of brown and gray facial hair, and his hair is short yet messy. He gives me a firm handshake, and I take half a second to inspect his numerous tattoos. "I'm Garth, Billie's dad. It's nice to finally meet you."

I blush. So Billie has talked about me? I wonder what she's said.

A door slams across the house, and Billie comes down the hallway, putting her short hair in a tiny ponytail.

"Dad, you'd better not be telling lies about me," she says. I'm instantly jealous at the obvious affection in Garth's eyes for his daughter. My dad still hasn't called me back.

"Don't worry," he replies with an easy smile. "I was just telling her that you and Doris are both goblins and that she should run."

Billie rolls her eyes, and Garth gives her a giant kiss on the cheek.

"Dad," she cries, her face turning bright pink. This is probably the first time I've seen her without makeup, which means I finally see that she has a smattering of freckles across her cheeks. I wonder how much else I have yet to learn. She looks at me. "We can go in my room." Her voice is good-natured despite her obvious embarrassment.

"Leave the door open," her dad says, a hint of warning in his voice.

"Dad, oh my god!" she says, leading me down the hall. I'm either excited or anxious, but either way, my stomach is filled to the brim with butterflies.

Billie's room surprises me. I'd expected theatre posters and a messy bedspread, but everything looks organized and precise. Instead of posters, she has a few floral prints on the wall, and her bed has a plain teal comforter and matching pillows. There's a white desk in the corner, but she doesn't have photos or decorations on it, just a plain black laptop that's shut. The room looks more like a guest room.

"Wow," I say. "I feel bad about how messy my room always is."

Billie laughs. "Don't. I cleaned like a maniac when you texted me. If you open my closet, you'll stop being my friend."

I laugh, although there isn't a lot of feeling in it. How am I supposed to tell this incredible girl how I feel? I haven't dated anyone in a while, and I can't imagine how she might react to the news. There should really be classes on this sort of thing.

"Ugh, I cannot go to work today," she says, lying back on the bed. I sit in the desk chair, straddling it backwards and resting my head on my crossed arms. "We've got a new guy, and he will not stop hitting on customers. It's basically the worst."

"Sounds gross," I agree, my hands tensing over the back of the chair. The words repeat over and over in my head. Billie, I have feelings for you. I have for a long time. Since I moved here, in fact. I keep getting ready to open my mouth to say the words, but the idea of actually saying them out loud is paralyzing.

"I mean, it's not the absolute worst thing. I kid you not, some toddler took a crap on the floor two weeks ago. Thank god I wasn't working that day."

"Oh my god," I say. Billie, I have feelings for you. Romantic feelings.

"Yeah, working in any sort of customer service

is the freaking worst," she says, rolling onto her stomach to make eye contact with me, dragging a pillow from the head of the bed so she has something to rest on. I nod in agreement, although I haven't actually had a job before. Mom and Dad both think I should focus more on school.

Oh, god, I've just been sitting here staring at her for a full minute. Is she expecting me to reply? I open my mouth, but Billie speaks before I can.

"Kaylee told me you like me," she says, planting her face into a pillow immediately after. Her voice is muffled as she continues, "I know it was probably just to cover up for the dragon thing, but I've been wanting to ask you about it."

Wait, what?

When did I...?

I think back and vaguely recall the conversation with Kaylee, the one right after Billie caught me with Maximus.

I speak slowly, considering each word before letting it out. "I did just say that because of you finding Maximus," I say, "But that doesn't make it untrue."

Billie looks up at me, her mouth a half frown. Yup, I've definitely screwed this up. There's no way she feels the same.

"It's true? Like, you actually like me?" She pauses. "Romantically?" I close my eyes and nod. My breath has all gone out of me. I want nothing more than to hide. "Because I also...have feelings...for you." Her words are careful and stilted, and my eyes snap open.

"You do?" I ask, the words making some sort of sense in my head. I smile slowly, but my heart is still racing with fear.

"Yeah," she says, her voice small.

"Well. That's...good," I say. The tightness in my chest finally releases as I come to terms with what we've both admitted. My voice is more enthusiastic when I speak again. "No, that's awesome."

Billie smiles, and that simple expression breaks me down.

Chapter Twenty-Five
Billie

WE GO FOR A WALK AROUND THE neighborhood, our fingers brushing occasionally. My heart speeds up every time, and I can't stop smiling. We pass Kaylee's house, and then Filicia's shortly after, but neither of them appear to be home.

When we're almost back to my house and I've just about worked up the courage to lace my fingers through Theo's, I get an image from Filicia. When I open it my mouth goes dry. In the photo, Maximus is crouched in the far corner of a wire dog kennel, his mouth open in a hiss and his wings extended to make him appear bigger. Guess what we caught??? Time to go dragon hunting! Tom's caption reads.

"What is it?" Theo asks, but I can't look at her. I just keep staring at the photo.

She takes my phone, then covers her mouth and cries out.

"Dad," I yell, my voice hoarse through the lump forming in my throat. He comes out on the porch without putting on shoes.

He takes us in for a minute before saying, "What's going on?" He grips the side railing, his knuckles going white.

I explain, "Tom and Kayden found the baby dragon. He got out, and they caught it. They're going to use it as bait to lure out the rest."

"Wait, dragon?" Dad asks, but he slips on his boots right inside the front door and grabs his keys. "Get in the car. You can explain on the way."

It doesn't slip my notice that Theo hasn't spoken since she saw the picture. I drag her to the truck, and we sit in the backseat. Doris runs out of the house. "Wait for me!" she calls, hopping on one foot as she forces her other sneaker on. She jumps into the passenger seat, straightening her cap, and Dad pulls out of the driveway, the wheels skidding over gravel.

Theo's phone starts to ring, and she answers. "Nana, what happened?"

I can't make out the words on the other line, but the voice is definitely distressed.

"Someone caught him," she replies. "We're going to find him now."

She hangs up without saying goodbye, which gives me palpitations just thinking about doing something like that to somebody.

It's not hard to tell where Tom has gone. The further into town we get, the more cars we encounter. When we get into downtown Bore's Grove, there's so much traffic that Dad has to stop the car. I jump out, and Theo follows me. We follow the flow of others who've also left their vehicles, and I can't see a thing.

We shove to the front of the crowd. Everyone in town must be here, bodies pressed thick against us, and my breathing comes in short, shallow gasps. Thankfully, Theo isn't afraid to use her elbows to force people to move away from us. When we reach the center of the square, Tom is sitting in the bed of his old pickup truck, a crowbar in hand and Maximus in a cage.

"Who's ready to end this reign of terror?" Kayden shouts, standing atop the roof of the truck, his face manic.

Everyone cheers, and I frown. This is wrong. Everything about this is wrong. Maximus hisses at Tom, who taps the cage with the crowbar, a ring resonating over the crowd. Maximus flinches, shutting his mouth and crouching lower to the floor of the kennel.

"You're the one who started this!" Theo screams, and I look up at her in awe. How is she so confident? "It's your fault the dragon attacked the city in the first place!"

Kayden's smile falters for just an instant, but when he focuses on Theo's face, he laughs. "You have no idea what you're talking about. You're not even from here." Someone shoves her from behind, and she stumbles out onto the grass. I spin around to see who did it, but there are too many people to determine.

I grit my teeth and go forward, helping Theo to stand. She raises a middle finger to Kayden and Tom. "You're both pieces of shit," she says. Then, she does something even I can't anticipate. She lunges forward, reaching for the kennel door. Is she going to try to free Maximus?

Tom sees it coming, though, and waves a hand at her. A blast of wind knocks her right back to the ground, and I catch a slight flicker of electricity in her clenched fists.

Before she can try again, a siren blares.

Thank God, the police, I think.

When Chief Trotter comes to the front of the crowd with a bullhorn, though, my heart sinks. Why does it have to be him? He's the only person in this town that might make this whole situation worse.

"This is an inappropriate display, young men," he says. "You're blocking traffic and causing a disruption. I suggest you come with me to the station."

I sigh with relief. Has he finally come to his senses?

Tom and Kayden's faces fall, but they agree to go with him. Good. This will all be over.

"What about Max—" Theo stutters. "The dragon? What's going to happen with him?"

Chief Trotter looks at the truck, at the dragon hunched in the kennel.

"We'll figure something out," he says.

Chapter Twenty-Six
Theo

A S IT TURNS OUT, "FIGURING SOME-
thing out" means a city council discussion.
Billie has to work all weekend, so I'm stuck lying
in my room and twiddling my thumbs, awaiting
news.

"Theo?" Mom says, knocking on my door lightly as she opens it. When she sees me still curled up
beneath my comforter, she frowns. "I was thinking
about going to get some ice cream, do you want to
go?"

I'm about to tell her that I'd rather eat a bucket
of bees than get ice cream with her, but I remem-

ber Nana's words from the other day. And the fact that, while Mom hasn't been easy to be around, at least she's been there.

"Sure," I say. "That sounds nice."

I don't change out of my pajamas, and Mom doesn't comment on my attire as we climb into her orange corvette.

I chew my lip as we sit in silence. When we pull into the drive-through to find a line, I finally ask, "Why did you and Dad separate?"

Mom looks at me in shock. Granted, these are the most words I've spoken to her in the months since we left New York. She opens her mouth, then closes it, her eyes pained.

Eventually, she says, "I don't want to speak ill of your father."

I let out a sharp laugh. "I think I can handle it."

She watches me for a moment, then looks forward. We pull up by another space, and she sighs. "He was cheating on me."

This is not the answer I expected.

"I knew about it, but I thought we could work through it. But when I was also…unfaithful…we decided it was best to end things."

Wait, what?

I have so many questions, but the one I choose is, "Who were you with?"

Mom lets out a humorless laugh. "You will not believe this."

"Try me," I say. I'm still trying to process her confession, and I don't think I can handle any deep questions about emotions or motives.

She looks at me, her eyebrows raised. "Jim, the guy from the gym."

My eyes widen. "The weird hipster guy with that god-awful mustache?"

Mom laughs again. "It wasn't that bad. And he was nice."

I roll my eyes. "If by 'not that bad' you mean terrible, and 'nice' you mean skeevy, then sure!"

"At least it wasn't Janice," she says, her voice filled with clear distaste.

"Wait. Wait. Secretary Janice? That's so cliche!" I burst into a fit of giggles, and Mom follows. It's finally our turn to order, and she has to speak through bursts of laughter. Tears stream down my face, icy with the cold breeze from the open window.

When we pull away from the ordering box, though, my tears won't stop. I suck in a breath, and it catches in my throat. A sob comes out instead of a normal breath out.

Mom's hand rests on my shoulder, and she pays for our ice cream quietly. Instead of driving home, she pulls off into a parking spot.

"I do want you to know," she says, "that none of this was your fault. Your father and I both love you very much, and none of our mistakes will change that."

My whole body shudders, and tiny sparks fly out of my fingertips. I sit on my hands so Mom doesn't see.

"He hasn't called me since we moved," I say, my voice thick with tears. I have to sniff so I don't snot all over myself.

"I'm so sorry, Theo." She sets the ice cream on the dashboard and rubs my back. "I know this is hard for you. I can't imagine what you must be going through."

I suck. In a deep breath, trying to steady myself.

"Thanks." My voice is tiny, like I'm a little kid again. Mom wraps an arm around me, and I lay my head on her shoulder. "I'm sorry I've been such a gremlin."

Mom laughs, but when I look up at her, there are tears in her eyes. "No," she says. "You've been great. And the worst thing you've done is hide a dragon in your room."

I sit up and look at her through the corner of my eye. "You know about that?"

She waves me off. "When I was your age, I was sneaking out and being a menace. Did you know I stole a car once?"

My eyes widen. "Mom!"

She laughs. "I returned it a few hours later. You know my mother would have killed me if I took her car, and I needed a ride."

I shake my head. "Christ, Mom."

She smiles for a moment longer, then her face goes serious again.

"But really, Theo. I'm proud of you."

I frown. "Thanks."

When we get home, I check online to find a new article. Apparently, there's going to be a city council meeting about what to do with the dragon later in the week. Wednesday afternoon.

As cathartic as the moment with Mom was, my mood instantly sours.

Chapter Twenty-Seven
Theo

TOWN HALL IS ABSOLUTELY PACKED. Half the town must be here, and Billie and I are forced to take a seat at the back. Nana makes her way to the front, side-eyeing Tom into giving her his seat. Nothing like using Southern values to get what you want.

"This meeting will now come to order," the man at the center says. He's a large man with a thick brown mustache, and I recognize him from the grocery store, because he always seems to be there when Nana goes shopping on Friday afternoons.

"We're here for an emergency session to discuss

the issue of the flock of dragons that have been seen outside of town," he says. "And the juvenile dragon that was captured earlier in the week. If anyone would like to speak, please form a line toward the podium."

Several people rush the stand, and Chief Trotter ends up being the first up. I grimace but don't move.

"Along with many people in this town," he says, "I believe that the dragons are a menace. We've been terrorized by this flock of mountain dragons for far too long, and I think you can agree with me that using the baby dragon to draw them out is an opportunity we shouldn't pass up."

The man at the front of the room nods along, but his face doesn't belay any information.

The next few people in line seem to agree with him, and then it's Nana's turn.

"I would like to respectfully disagree," she says, and the room goes dead silent as all ears are trained on her. "I found this baby dragon in my yard, and it has already been arranged for him to be released into the care of a rescue organization. I believe that these actions are causing a lot of undue stress to this creature, when instead we should do what we've been told and hope that the flock moves on. They aren't harming anyone."

When she sits, Tom is the next up. "With all due respect, ma'am, one of those dragons almost killed someone at the Dragon's Day parade. The only reason it didn't is because someone killed it, and I'm glad they did."

Way to take away Billie's act of heroism. When I look at her, Billie's jaw ticks. She stands and makes her way to the podium, taking the microphone away from Tom. A few people protest, but the city council doesn't say anything about her disruption.

"With all due respect, Tom," she says, and I wonder if everyone else can hear the mocking in her tone, "I'm the one who killed the dragon, and the only reason I did it was so that it wouldn't harm my..." She pauses, turning so her eyes lock on mine. She wavers for just a moment. "Friend," she decides. "And I don't believe that there's any reason to fear the rest of the dragons, especially because they've never come into town unprovoked.

There are so many statistics backing up that dragons just don't attack people for no reason. I believe that the female that landed in the square only did it to find her baby, and the attack five years ago was because certain people —" at this, she makes eye contact with Kayden, "—slaughtered its baby in cold blood."

At that, a mumble sweeps through the room, but Chief Trotter stands and points at her. "You have no evidence to support this claim," he says. "I suggest you watch what you're insinuating."

Billie almost responds, but she bites her tongue.

After taking a deep breath, she says one final sentence. "You're all the real monsters here." At that, she walks away from the stand and strides right out the door, leaving the room in a stunned silence.

I would go after her, but I have to know the council's decision. After several more people give their opinions, and some deliberating, the lead councilman leans into his microphone and says, "We will take the baby dragon to the locations where dragons have been spotted. After they are located, the baby will be released into the care of this," he gestures at Nana, "rescue organization."

With that, my world crashes around me.

Chapter Twenty-Eight
Billie

I DON'T SEE THEO AFTER THE CITY COUN-
cil meeting. I wait for her to call or text or something, but she doesn't. Instead, I see her in Interp
the next day, her entire body sullen.

"I heard what happened," I say after approaching her.

She shrugs. "I mean, it's not like I could've done
anything about it anyway. People in this town
just don't give a shit about anything except themselves."

I consider pointing out the few people that sup-
ported her side in the meeting, but I don't say any-

thing. She's hurting right now, and she probably just needs to vent.

"I'm glad they're finally doing something," Tom cuts in, twisting in his desk to look right at us. "Those bastards killed Matt, and a hell of a lot of other people."

"Oh, you mean Matt the rapist?" I spit back.

Immediately, he gets defensive. "Nobody proved anything, and that girl pulled her testimony."

"Because her family was threatened! Didn't you see how many cops showed up at her house?" My voice is quickly reaching catastrophic levels, and I am completely ready to destroy Tom in every way.

Nielsen shouts. "Children! Work on your pieces or you'll all be in detention. I could really use someone to sort the costume closet!"

That shuts Tom up, and he simmers in his seat.

I turn back to Theo, although I lower my voice so Tom can't hear me this time. "It's going to be okay. Maximus is gonna be fine, and I'm sure he'll love the zoo."

Theo's eyes are daggers, and my heart stutters.

"That's not fine," she says. "They're going to kill the dragons, and you don't even care. Hell, I bet you're happy about it."

I lean back in my chair. She's just hurting. "You know that's not true," I mumble. My heart twinges.

She rolls her eyes. "Please. You hate the dragons more than anyone in this awful town. You're just as bad as the rest of them."

Where the hell is this coming from? "You know, I'm one of the only people who took your side, so if you actually think that about me, you can fuck right off." I stand from my chair and grab my backpack. To Nielsen, I say, "I'm going to practice in the auditorium. Get some peace and quiet."

I stomp across the hall and fling the auditorium door open, stalking backstage to hide behind the curtains. Instead of practicing my piece, though, I sit on the ground, resting my face on my knees. A tinny alarm goes off on my phone, and I check it to see that it's almost time for my NYU audition. Great. Just fucking great. With everything going on, I'd completely forgotten about it, and now I'll be a horrible mess performing my dramatic piece for a committee of the harshest judges in the world.

I set up my phone on a spare tripod for the meeting and turn on the stage lights so they'll be able to see me. When the call comes in, I introduce myself and perform my piece to the best of my abilities, though my hands are shaking and my lungs are tight. When it's finished, a woman with a tight bun says, "Thank you. We'll be in touch." Her face is completely flat, but I thank her and hang up.

There goes my entire future.

Chapter Twenty-Nine
Billie

FOR THE FIRST TIME SINCE SCHOOL START-
ed, Doris and I are both at Mom's apartment in Gatlinburg. Until now, I've been too busy with the play and debate tournaments. It's a small place with two bedrooms, so Doris and I have bunk beds in our room. I'm working on my homework on the couch, and Doris is sulking in our room because she didn't get to go to the aquarium today. It doesn't help that Mom made a snarky comment about Doris's "boy clothes."

"I'm thinking about ordering a pizza," Mom says, crashing onto the couch next to me and crinkling my History assignment about the Florida Magic Wars of the 1880's. "Oops, sorry," she says, pulling it out and doing her best to smooth it on the table.

I roll my eyes. She turns on the TV, scrolling until she finds a show about dragon trainers.

"Can we watch something else?" I ask in a deadpan voice.

She hands me the remote, and I click the first interesting thing to come up, which happens to be Queer Eye.

"Ugh," she says. "Speaking of gay guys, has your dad been screwing anyone lately?"

I grit my teeth as she laughs at her own terrible joke. Is it even a joke or is she just trying to be mean?

"Seriously, I can't believe he had to go and choose men over me. Like, I was so bad that he changed sides completely."

I try to block her out, but she just keeps talking.

"I would understand if he'd cheated on me, but deciding he was gay? I can't believe it."

This is why I never come to Mom's house. I slam

my pencil on the table and spin to her.

"Mom, you have to shut up. Seriously. People don't decide they're gay. They just are."

Mom rolls her eyes, ignoring my anger. "Sure, whatever. Take his side. I get it. Guess I'm just not PC enough for you."

At that, I snap. "Have you ever considered that maybe one of your kids could be gay? And that's why I take Dad's side?"

Mom looks suddenly confused. "Doris isn't gay." I don't ask how she can be sure about that. Whatever Doris is going through isn't my place.

I raise my eyebrows and wait for her mind to catch up with her mouth.

The moment it clicks, her jaw drops.

"And there it is," I say like an announcer. "You heard it here, folks, Lori Walker has just discovered that her daughter is a big old lesbian." Perhaps I shouldn't be so cavalier about all this, but I can't help it. It's like all my stress from the last few weeks has built up inside me, and Mom's homophobia was the straw that broke the camel's back.

She chews her lip. "Is this because of your dad?"

I gasp out a laugh. "No, Mom. Dad being gay did not turn me gay. I have been gay forever, and I will be gay forever." I wave my hand at her and pack up my homework. "You know what? I'm going for a walk. It's getting a bit stuffy in here."

I don't wait for Mom to reply. I just get up and leave. Dad is supposed to be picking us up at six anyway, so it's not like I have to wait long. If I can just stay out for a couple hours, I'll be fine.

By the time I make it down the hill, my anger has run out. I sit at a bench in front of a touristy shop, pulling my phone out to scroll through Facebook. There's nothing interesting going on there, and I consider texting Theo before remembering that she apparently hates me now.

When I set my phone down at five-thirty, I look up to see Mom walking down the hill toward me. She's going slowly, and when her eyes catch mine, she hesitates, almost like she's gathering her courage.

She doesn't sit on the bench with me. Instead, she stands in front of me on the sidewalk. I shiver at a breeze that sweeps through, and she passes me a pair of gloves from her coat pocket. I hesitate but end up taking them anyway.

"I'm sorry I hurt your feelings," Mom finally says. She looks back up the hill toward the apartment. "I shouldn't have made jokes like that about your father. No matter what I think, he's still your dad."

I look away. That's not a real apology. She isn't apologizing for her cutting words, just for the fact that I heard them. "It's fine," I lie.

She finally sits, leaning against me. "I still love you," she says. "Nothing will change that."

Somehow, I don't believe her. The lack of a real apology makes all her words ring false. However, I'm too tired to fight anymore. I just want to go home and not have to deal with this anymore.

"I applied to NYU," I say to change the subject. "My audition was this week. Ms. Nielsen thinks I have a good chance at a scholarship."

"That's great." She doesn't sound interested anymore, and she's pulling out her phone. "Was that a yes on pizza?"

I sigh. Nothing I say will make this woman give a shit. "Sure."

Chapter Thirty
Theo

IT'S SUNDAY EVENING, AND INSTEAD OF finishing the stack of homework on my desk, I'm standing in city hall, my fingers laced through the bars of the cage that Maximus is trapped inside. At least now he has a small bowl of water and some food. Better than Tom and Kayden did for him.

He cries at me to be let out, but there's a spell on the cage that makes freeing him impossible. "I'm sorry," I say. Tears prick at my eyes.

The door to the building opens, but I ignore it. Probably just a janitor. Anybody can be in City

Hall whenever.

"I thought I might find you here," Billie says. I don't turn around. She continues, "I wanted to apologize for yelling at you the other day. I shouldn't have gotten so angry. I'm really sorry."

I look down, a tear falling and splashing on the cold concrete floor.

"It's fine," I say. I've regretted my words to her ever since I said them.

"No, it's not," she says. "I know you didn't mean what you said, but I got angry and hurt you. I just wanted to let you know that I was wrong."

How did she even find me here? Can't she see that I want to be alone?

"I was wrong, too," I whisper. "I said some awful things. I'm sorry."

Now leave me alone. But I don't speak the words aloud.

Billie joins me by the cage, but she doesn't speak, which I appreciate. She puts a hand up to the cage, and Maximus comes up to sniff her. She scratches his snout, and he purrs.

I shift my weight so I'm just a little closer to Billie, and she does the same. Our shoulders are now touching. I tilt my head, and it rests on Billie's.

Maximus chirps, and I rub his wing with a finger. My other hand brushes against Billie's and she takes it, lacing our fingers together.

I sigh. "Everything is kind of shit right now, isn't it?"

She pulls away from me slightly, but our hands are still intertwined. She looks into my eyes, and hers are stormy. "Not everything."

I smile halfheartedly. "Right. Not everything."

If nothing else is going right, then at least we have this moment, our hearts at rest and our hands together.

After a moment, Billie gasps. "I have an idea," she says. She releases my hand and digs her phone out of her pocket. I'm about to ask what she's doing when she makes a call.

"Hey, I need you guys to meet at my house in twenty minutes. It's an emergency." After she says goodbye, she looks up at me, her face aglow.

"What's going on?" I ask. The complete three-sixty in her mood has me wary.

She grins. "We're going to save the dragons. All of them."

Chapter Thirty-One
Billie

WHEN WE ARRIVE AT MY HOUSE, FILI-cia's car is parked next to Dad's in the driveway. I lead Theo inside, and I ignore the pointed stares at our intertwined hands. This is not what we're here to discuss. There are more important matters at hand.

"What's going on?" Kaylee asks from her position on the armchair, one leg over the side and the other over the back of the chair. There's no way that can be comfortable, but I don't question it.

I breathe out. I still haven't told Filicia or Kaylee about Maximus, but it's time to come clean. I explain everything, from Theo finding him in her pool all the way to the town meeting. I skim over the more gruesome parts of the video we found, although I'm sure they'll both want to see it later. Right now, though, there's no time.

"Holy shit," Filicia says.

At that moment, Dad walks in the room.

"Did I hear that you've been keeping a dragon in your home?" he asks. Einstein pads in after him and hops on the couch, resting his head in Filicia's lap.

Theo nods.

"So what's the plan?" he asks. "They're going out to hunt the dragons tonight."

We look at each other, then back to Dad. "I was kind of hoping you could help, actually."

We gather in the living room, and Kaylee makes sure we have plenty of snacks while we're planning. With Dad's experience as a park ranger, tracking down the dragons should be a lot easier. All we have to do is get Maximus and use him to lure the flock out of town, although the logistics of it are harder than expected.

At nine o'clock, I check Instagram to find that Tom posted three minutes ago, this time a selfie of himself holding a gun in front of Maximus's cage.

Time to slay some dragons!

I grit my teeth. "It's time," I say. "Remember, if we get separated, we have three meeting points depending on what time it is."

We split into two groups. I'm going to be in Dad's car, and everyone else is with Filicia. As everyone else is loading up, Theo pulls me to the side on the front porch.

"In case anything goes wrong," she says, her eyes downcast. Quick as lightning, she leans forward and presses her lips to mine. Before I can even absorb what's going on, though, the kiss is over. I open my mouth to speak, but she shakes her head. "There's no time."

I swallow and nod. When we separate into different vehicles, I stare at her until the door is closed.

The night is pitch black and charged with an energy I've never felt before.

Please let this go well.

Chapter Thirty-Two
Theo

THERE'S A WHOLE LINE OF CARS GOING up the mountain road out of town. Garth's SUV is ahead of us, and every now and then, I catch the taillights of another car or two further up. When the road turns to gravel, though, Garth's tail lights disappear. Filicia flicks a switch on her dashboard, and our lights turn off, too. Now, we've only got the light of the moonless stars to guide us, but we can't risk being seen.

The SUV darts off on a side road to the right, and I try to catch a glimpse of Billie in the passenger seat, but it's far too dark for that. We continue up the road. If all goes well, we should be back together within the hour. If it goes wrong…

I shake the thought away. I can't think like that. This has to go smoothly, and I have no time for negative thoughts if I want this to work.

We have to avoid getting too close to the rest of the cars, as we don't want to be seen. They turn onto a dirt road to the left, and we follow.

"This only goes up like a mile," Filicia says. "But there's another dirt path for Jeeps and stuff. Most of the cars in the convoy can't make it there, but that's where Billie and Garth will be coming out."

I nod. This had all been explained in the house, but I pay close attention anyway. When the cars are just barely in sight, Filicia pulls off to the side, the car at a dangerously steep angle.

"Won't they see your taillights?" I ask.

Filicia laughs. "The headlights have to be on for the taillights to work."

Wow. This is not a safe car to be in. "Great," I say, my voice about an octave too high for the word.

We clamber out carefully, and I have to steady myself against a tree trunk to avoid sliding down the hill. It's quite a hike to the hunting party, but it's better than the risk of being seen.

Thankfully, the plan is working so far. When we catch up with them, they're all parked in disarray. Garth's SUV is at the head of the path, hood open and smoke pouring out. He's saying something to Chief Trotter, who's at the lead of the group. Garth gestures wildly, but Billie is no longer in the car. A tap on my shoulder startles me, and I have to hold in a scream. When I look, though, it's just Billie, hiding in the brush. She'd ridden with Garth to give him directions with the hiking map so they didn't fly off the side of the mountain in the pitch black.

"—think it's my radiator," Garth says, a sentence we've been waiting to hear.

"Go," Billie whispers, and I stumble forward as quietly as possible through the thick underbrush.

Most of the people are out of their cars, prepping their weapons or listening to Garth. Through all of this, Maximus has been left unattended.

When we get up to the back of the truck, I reach up to the cage, and a hand grabs my wrist.

"What the —" Tom says, but before he can bring attention to us, I do something I've been holding in for months. I focus all my energy on that hand, and a jolt of electricity runs through and drops him right to the ground.

Billie looks from me to him, then back to me.

"Nice trick," she just says, then mumbles a few words to break the less extreme spell on Maximus's cage. He immediately climbs onto her shoulder, and she smiles. This is going well so far. We just have to get away now.

A yell and a grunt causes both of us to turn back to the commotion, though. Garth is against his car, Chief Trotter pressing him up and wrapping him in handcuffs.

Billie moves like she's going to help, but I grab her hand.

"There's nothing we can do," I whisper. "He'll be fine, but we have to go now."

Billie takes one last look at her father, then scrunches her eyes shut before turning around and escaping into the woods.

Chapter Thirty-Three
Billie

WE'VE DONE MOST OF IT, BUT WE LOST Dad in the process. My eyes sting, and my breath is coming in short, shallow gasps. When we all pile into Filicia's car, I say, "What are we gonna do? We can't find them without Dad."

Theo puts a hand on my back and moves it in gentle circles. "It's okay. It'll be fine."

She's lying. Her voice is laced with false hope, and I hang my head. "We shouldn't have tried. This was a bad idea. What if he's hurt?"

Kaylee cuts in. "He'll be okay. Chief Trotter is a dick, but he's not gonna hurt someone. We just have to focus on finding the dragons."

I nod, although I don't know how we're going to accomplish such a monumental task, especially not in the middle of the night.

A low keen reverberates through the car, and I almost think that I've started crying. I shut my mouth, but the sound doesn't stop.

"What's he doing?" Filicia asks, her eyes wide.

Theo tilts her head. "I think he might be…calling for them? Or something?" She's as unsure as the rest of us, though.

"Should we get out of the car?" Kaylee asks, looking around. She opens the door, and a matching sound floats in from up the mountain.

They're close.

We scramble out of the car—it's not like we can take it up the blocked pathway, anyway—and begin the trek back through the trees. We keep a wide berth around the commotion, although Dad is nowhere in sight. I cross my fingers that he's just hidden in the back of the police car rather than brutalized by the angry crowd. People are shouting at each other, planning. This has to go fast, or we're going to lose our opportunity.

They still have to get Dad's car out of the way, which I'm sure will be harder without the starter cable buried in my coat pocket. We manage to get around them before hiking up the back trail. When we're far enough, Filicia snaps her fingers, and tiny violet and pink lights glow along the path ahead of us, each one blinking out as we reach it.

Maximus keens again, but this time, the response comes quick and loud. How long have we been walking? I freeze and look around, but all I see are trees. We can't be far from the rest of the flock, though. Not with how loud that sound was.

"It's alright, boy," Theo mumbles, patting him. "We're almost there."

I shiver. I've only just gotten used to being around Maximus. There's no telling how I'll respond to seeing fully grown dragons. Will they try to eat us? I swallow the fear, and it settles deep in the pit of my stomach. We're probably not going to die tonight. I hope.

A moment later, the call stops, and Filicia's lights go out.

My eyes try to adjust to the darkness, but with the thick coniferous trees enveloping us, there's no light to guide us.

I open my mouth to ask the group what we should do, but a huff of breath stops me.

It came from my left, and it was far too large to be any of us.

I squeeze my eyes shut, and I grab Theo's hand, tightening my fingers around hers. I can't breathe. Who would have thought that I'd die by suffocating from fear the next time I came into contact with mountain dragons?

A rumble shakes me to my core, but I don't move. Maybe if I stay still, it won't be able to see me. I remember hearing that in a movie once.

"Holy shit," Kaylee breathes.

Maximus chirps, and a moment later, he's gone from my shoulder. I've never seen him fly, but he didn't climb off me.

I open my eyes and regret it immediately. Inches from my face, Maximus is staring at me through a cage of bared teeth that are as long as my forearm. Another breath huffs out, blasting my hair back, and I stumble backwards. Theo doesn't move.

Another chirp catches my attention, and I catch another set of eyes staring at me from the dragon's mouth. How many babies does it have in there?

Theo laughs breathily. "There's a whole clutch of them."

The adult swings its head around, and I strain my ears and eyes. What could possibly be startling this creature? Then, I hear it. Pickup engines and tires on gravel.

"They're coming," Filicia says.

I take a slow step toward the dragon. I've heard that the larger breeds of dragons are extremely intelligent, and that some can even understand some English.

"There's danger," I say slowly. "You have to get out of here."

It turns back to me, its mouth hanging slightly open to accommodate the babies in its maw.

"I don't think—" Theo says, but I interrupt her.

"They're going to kill you. Like they did..." I suck in a shuddering breath, then let it out slowly. "Like I did. Before. I'm sorry. But you have to go now." Desperation seeps into the cracks of my voice, and the dragon arches its head. A high whine comes out, and another dragon comes out of the trees. How many are hiding in there?

Arthur crawls out of its mouth and lands on my shoulder, and I flinch as the adult jerks its head in surprise. Please don't eat me, I beg in my mind. It doesn't, though. It merely cocks its head.

"I think we should show them," Theo says. "Maybe if we lead them out of town, the hunters won't be able to follow."

I grit my teeth. There aren't really any other options. "Okay," I say, then sigh. "Alright. Um. Fly, I guess." I wrap my arms around Maximus, and he squeaks at me. "And follow us."

When the dragons launch themselves into the sky, the wind from their wings like tornado gusts, Theo pulls me by my hand, and we race back down the mountain.

Chapter Thirty-Four
Billie

WE HAVE TO SNEAK AROUND THE convoy, and they don't appear to notice us or the dragons. At least we have the cover of darkness to protect us. When someone grabs my shoulder, I let out half a scream, but a hand slaps over my mouth.

"Billie, quiet," Dad says, and I squint to see his face in the dark. "Get to the truck. We've got to get to the park, and I'm not sure her car can make it that far."

Filicia frowns at the insinuation. "Fair," she says. "Rude, but fair."

"They know you took Maximus. They're trying to find you now. We have to go right now, or it'll be trouble." That's when his pale face finally becomes clear enough for me to see in the darkness, along with the blood marring his nose and lips.

We go to the SUV, Theo keeping watch while I hide in the back with Maximus. When I glance at the sky, dark yet distant shapes block out the stars with slow sweeps. Maximus makes his low keening sound yet again, and the dragons dotting the night bank just as Dad starts the car. Everyone clambers inside, and we peel out, this time taking the main road down. It's safer than the back trail we'd taken earlier, and far faster with how Dad drives.

"Nobody is following us," Kaylee says after a few minutes. She's in the middle row, and Filicia is up front with Dad. After Kaylee says that, she begins to fiddle with the radio until it manages to play soft music off her phone.

I smile and lean to rest my head on Theo's shoulder. She rubs her thumb over mine, and Maximus stretches out to lie across both our laps.

We did it. We actually did it. However, I didn't realize how exhausting it would be. My eyes drift shut. Maybe I could rest them for just a moment.

When Dad slams on the brakes, though, I jerk back into total consciousness, my eyes snapping open and Maximus flying off my lap and onto the floor.

"What's going on?" I ask, looking around blearily before I notice the flashing lights on the road ahead of us. There's only one way out of Bore's Grove, the state highway that winds through the mountains toward the interstate and then, even further, the national park where Dad works.

This is bad. This is really really really bad.

The barricade is made up of a few wooden barriers and three police cars. As we creep closer, figures materialize in the darkness, hardly discernible past the flashing blue and red.

We're trapped. And we have Maximus, which means the flock won't leave. By keeping him with us to lead them away, we've doomed them to certain death.

Dad stops before we're too close. "Stay in the

car," he says, his voice hard. As soon as he's out, though, the rest of us follow. We stand in a line, and Maximus uses Theo as a perch. "Let us through," Dad calls to the people at the barricade.

The voice that replies has me gritting my teeth. "Can't do that, I'm afraid," Tom says. "Give us the dragon, and you'll be free to go."

"No," I say. I try to muster up the confidence that Theo always seems to possess. I may not be tall, but I roll my shoulders back and stand with my legs apart, planting them and imagining that I'm an immovable boulder. I will not budge here.

"Billie, stop being stupid," Tom calls. "Just do what I say."

That was the wrong thing to say. If I see him at school tomorrow, I'm going to lay his ass out for everyone to see. Or maybe I'll get the chance to do it tonight, if it comes to that.

A rumble like thunder rolls through the clear sky above us, and a shotgun cocks from the line. I tense, but the dragons are too far up for anyone to be able to shoot them. I look down at our line, and pride swells in my chest. We are stiff and steady, an impassable army. Filicia holds her phone in one hand, recording this whole encounter. She thinks of absolutely everything.

"I think you ought to move," Theo says. "Our friends are bigger than your guns."

"Is that a threat?" Chief Trotter's voice replies. So he hadn't gone on with the hunting party. When Dad escaped, he must have gotten an idea of our plan.

"No," Theo says nonchalantly. "Just a fact. It's not like we have any control over two-hundred ton wild animals."

Her hand tightens in mine, and it's trembling, but her voice is steady. If we survive this, I'm going to kiss her until neither of us can think anymore.

They don't respond for a while, but Chief Trotter gives way first. "Put your guns down," he orders. The two officers with him lower their hands, but Tom doesn't put away his shotgun. "Tom, now."

Still, though, Tom doesn't move. He lowers the gun, but not completely. He brings it from the dragons in the sky to aiming it directly at Theo. Or, more accurately, Maximus. Still, a shotgun at that distance would kill them both.

"Put the gun down, son," Dad calls. A screech careens from the sky, and I put my hands on my ears at the exact moment that the world explodes.

Chapter Thirty-Five
Theo

I'M NOT DEAD. I HAVE TO PAT MYSELF down, but I really haven't been shot. Still, I'm on the ground, and Billie is pulling at me, begging me to stand. Her Dad is yelling something, and Filicia and Kaylee are holding Tom to the ground at the barrier. How did they get way over there? I stumble to my feet, but everything seems too bright, and the sounds are too distant.

"We have to go!" she shouts, but the sound is miles away.

I let her pull me away, although my eyes trace

the trees that are lit like torches in the night. Billie helps me into the SUV, but nobody else is following us. She gets in the driver's seat and starts it up.

"What about everyone else?" I ask, my mouth made of cotton.

"They'll be fine," she says through gritted teeth. It takes a moment for me to absorb her words. We're leaving them behind?

Just then, red floods the sky like blood in the breeze, gold reflecting off it. It's one of the dragons, and it takes one of the cars in its talons and throws it into the trees. Holy shit, what is going on?

I'm thrown against the back of the seat as Billie guns it, and the SUV squeezes through the new space in the road. I spin around, and my ears ring as I watch the calamity fade into the distance. When we hit a curve, they're gone.

"I can't hear right," I say, trying to avoid shouting.

Billie's eyes are wide when she looks at me, but she nods. We don't speak through the rest of the car ride, and Maximus falls asleep in my lap, seemingly oblivious to the disaster that we just experienced.

We survived. In this moment, that's all that matters. Billie sets one hand on the center console, and I take it in mine. We're alive, and we're together.

I'VE ONLY BEEN TO THE NATIONAL PARK a few times. It's an hour through the winding mountains, but at least it's an easy drive. Theo doesn't release my hand for even a second.

"What do you think will happen to them?" I ask. Theo sets her jaw and doesn't respond. I nod. It's response enough.

I keep the window open, and every now and then, a dragon calls out. At least they're still following us. Maximus doesn't awaken the whole time.

"You know," Theo says, staring out her window, "I never thought about how beautiful it is here. I've been so upset about leaving New York that I never gave this place a chance."

I take a second to glance at her. "Yeah, I guess."

I've lived here my entire life. The furthest I've ever been from Bore's Grove was a trip to Nashville when I was six. Now, though, I stare out the windshield, trying to see it with her eyes.

Because there's no moon, the stars shine brighter than usual in the crisp night air, glowing against a blue and purple sky. The mountains are pitch black against this sight, staggered like an open maw. In my rearview mirror, the tiny pinprick lights of Bore's Grove glow the higher we get up the mountain, our little valley of golden lights in a dark world.

"What are we gonna do when we get back?" I ask.

Theo shakes her head. "Let's just focus on getting these guys to safety. We'll figure everything else out after that."

When we pull up to the closed gates, three park rangers are there to greet us. At least Dad called ahead to let them know we'd be here.

"Where's Garth?" a woman asks, shining her flashlight into the backseat as she props herself up against my window.

A pang resonates through my chest. "He caught caught up in town."

She frowns and nods. "I'm not sure what the state was thinking letting Bore's Grove try to hunt the dragons, but this kind of thing never ends well. I'm glad you were able to get them here."

At that moment, an electric shock runs through me, then another, then another.

"Six adult dragons," calls a man from the guard shack.

"What was that?" Theo asks, flexing her hands out in front of her and popping her jaw.

The woman laughs. "We have a barrier to keep protected wildlife in the park. It goes all the way down into Georgia, so they'll have plenty of space to roam, but we don't want them getting into any-more trouble. We're also able to keep track of their movements within the park."

I tilt my head. "That's pretty neat."

Theo and I get out of the SUV, passing Maximus over to another woman in a ranger uniform. We follow them into a building set a little back from the road, and the man at the guard shack waves at us with two fingers, leaning back in his tall rolling chair and propping his feet on the desk.

After all the darkness of the night, the fluorescents inside are blindingly bright. I have to stop and blink a few times just so I can actually see. I'd expected an office, but instead, we're in what appears to be a break room, sofas against the walls and a full kitchen setup.

The woman sets Maximus on a wooden table after tossing an old coffee cup in the trash. "Sorry about the mess," she says. Then, she goes over Maximus, running her hands over his wings and body, taking his temperature, and checking out the inside of his mouth. He doesn't seem pleased with that last one, but she's firm and forces him to keep his mouth open long enough for her to shine a flashlight down his throat. "He looks great," she says with surprise. "He's got a tiny amount of inflammation on his hydrogen glands, but other than that, he's in perfect health. I'm gonna give him an antibiotic, and then he'll be good to go."

She snaps her fingers, and a syringe is in her hand. She takes the cap off and puts it in the corner of Maximus's mouth, dispensing the white goop quickly. Maximus chomps his mouth and licks a few times, but at least he doesn't spit out the medicine.

"Good boy," she says, snapping her fingers once again. This time, the syringe is replaced with a small chunk of raw meat, and she tosses it for Maximus to catch in his mouth.

It's time to release him back into the wild.

Theo carries him outside, and he keens as soon as we step out the door. The returning keen is so much closer than I expect that I stumble, but I don't back down this time.

The dragons emerge from the trees, varying in size but all so much larger than I'm comfortable with. With all the lights around the ranger building, it's easy to make out all six dragons. If I'd seen this many when we found them in the woods earlier, I probably would've fainted like I had at the diner. Now, though, I just watch as Theo gets ready to pass Maximus off to the same dragon as earlier. It lowers its head and opens its mouth wide, and four more babies come bounding out, tripping over each other to get to the dirt.

Maximus chirps and leaps out of Theo's arms, joining the rest of his clutch.

I sigh and sit on the ground, which was apparently a mistake, as several very small and very sharp dragons go from attacking each other playfully to deciding that I'm the perfect perch. Their tiny claws dig past my thin jeans and prick at my skin, and I have to grit my teeth as one buries itself in my hair. "This is fine," I say, looking up to Theo. She bursts into laughter and sits next to me, taking one of them into her lap. With them all together, it's impossible to tell which is Maximus.

"I think he'll be fine," I say, cringing as another set of baby claws digs into my skin.

Theo nods, but a single tear streams down her cheek. "Yeah, I think so."

Chapter Thirty-Six
Theo

AFTER BILLIE AND I SKIP SCHOOL ON Monday to deal with the aftermath, we walk in to find an absolute madhouse when we return on Tuesday. Someone sticks their foot out to trip Billie as soon as we walk in, but I grab her around the waist to keep her from falling. At lunch, we sit with Kaylee and Filicia, who regale us with their mornings of dodging stray feet and other attacks. Kaylee even holds her hair out to reveal a chunk that was cut off by someone in her potions class.

"This is gonna be a fantastic year," Filicia says sarcastically. Something cold and wet moves down my back, and I spin around.

"Oops," a girl from theatre says with a smirk. "I accidentally spilled my milk down your back." She shrugs and walks away, her table snickering.

"What an asshole," Billie says. "Let's go to the bathroom. You can have my hoodie."

We walk there together, and I stare daggers at anyone who might even be thinking about doing something to us. Ever since Kayden was arrested for attempted murder, everyone hates our little group. If he weren't such a terrible shot, though, I'd be dead. He was arrested without bail, so at the very least, we won't be seeing him until his court date in December. I shiver at the thought that he might not be charged, though at least he won't be in the county for the trial, as it's a federal case.

I go into the far stall, and Billie sets her hoodie on top of the door. I pull off my soaked shirt and sports bra, then pull Billie's hoodie on. Immediately, her warmth and flowery scent envelopes me. I wrap my arms around myself for just a moment, then open the stall door to find her waiting for me.

"Thank you," I say.

Ever since Sunday night, we haven't done anything but hold hands. I wonder if she still wants anything to do with me, especially since I'm the one who everyone wants to get back at for pressing charges.

She takes my hand and takes a step toward me. I suddenly realize how perfectly alone we are in this bathroom. The heat from her body radiates toward me, and I shiver with anticipation.

"I think you should kiss me," she says, her voice slow and careful. Before I can think too much, I lean down and press my lips to hers. She throws her arms around my neck, and I wrap mine around her waist.

The kiss we'd shared on her porch had been quick and awkward, but now I realize that I have all the time in the world to explore this thing between us.

And her lips are so damn soft.

Chapter Thirty-Seven
Billie

WE SPEND AFTERNOONS AT THEO'S house. After the first week back at school, people get bored of tormenting us. There's too much else for them to focus on, like midterm exams and winter break plans. Theo and I almost have our Duo where we want it to be for the spring tournaments, although we spent a good deal of our time in her room making out. And we're only caught by her mom one of those times.

I avoid mentioning the upcoming court date, and we don't talk about the future. We don't have any idea where this relationship is going, and it's easier to just focus on how we feel right now.

The court date is the first day of winter break. That means that everyone is talking about it in school, and Theo and I come back into focus as the main targets of harassment, although Filicia and Kaylee don't have it much easier.

Mountain winters are frigid and unforgiving, and on my walk to school, a pickup drives by and crashes through a puddle, dousing me in icy water. I shiver the rest of the way there, although I'm lucky that there are extra theatre blacks in the costume closet.

It's going to be fine. We just have to survive today, and it will all be back to normal. Everyone will forget about this whole debacle over winter break.

As we're lining up to get into the end of semester assembly, my phone dings with an email. I glance at it when no teachers are looking, and my breath catches in my throat. It's from the NYU admissions team.

My breath is short, and I clutch my phone like a lifeline. I will not look at this. I will not spend my day moping about how I didn't get into their program and wondering what the hell I'm supposed to do after graduation.

I take a deep breath and sit as far over as possible. I catch Theo's athletic form halfway across the bleachers, but she doesn't spot me. A dull pain jumps into my back, and I twist around to find a few guys laughing among themselves. I set my jaw and ignore them. If they're going to kick me for doing what's right, then I'm not going to give them the benefit of a response.

There are plenty of the usual things in the assembly. The show choir performs, the band does a song, the principle does a speech, and there's a presentation with awards for people who do sports. I tune out pretty quickly to read a book, but when people start talking and getting restless, I look up to see what I've missed.

The principle appears to be panicking, and the projector is on. The gym's lights all turn off, and it takes my eyes a moment to absorb what's happening on the screen. When I realize, though, I gasp.

In the video, there are three boys, one of which is holding the camera. One of them kills a baby dragon for all to see.

The dragon chases them into town, but the video cuts off before one of the boys is killed. When the video turns off, the auditorium is dead silent. My eyes lock on where I'd seen Theo earlier, but she's gone.

Chapter Thirty-Eight
Billie

"YOU GOT MAIL FROM NYU," DAD SAYS casually when he picks me up. When I look at him, though, he seems confused. I wait for him to tell me off, to yell, to do something, but he just says, "I didn't know you were applying. What happened to Tenn Tech?"

My throat goes dry. "They don't have financial aid."

Dad nods, but his face falls even more. The past few years, he's always felt guilty about not having any sort of college savings for Doris and I. It breaks my heart that he feels this way.

"I didn't want you to feel bad," I say. "And I only applied to NYU because I was mad about tech school. There's no way I could get in to their theatre program."

"That's not true," Dad argues. "I've been to every play you've ever done, seen every perfor- mance you've had for competition. And I'm not just saying this because you're my daughter, but you're good." He stops at the one red light in town before turning right.

I don't reply. He says he's being unbiased, but how could he possibly be?

"I opened the letter," he says. I look at him, and my mouth falls open. No words come out. "You got in."

His words don't make any sense. It's not possi- ble. I'd totally bombed my audition. It's one of the most prestigious theatre programs in the country. I'm not good enough for something like that.

Dad pulls into the driveway and looks at me, placing a hand on my shoulder.

"Billie, I want you to know that I support you.

I know you picked that tech school because it was close and would keep you home, but we are going to be okay without you."

I shake my head. This can't be happening. This is a dream. It must be.

The corners of my eyes prick, and frigid tears run down my face.

Dad leans over the console and wraps me in a strong hug. He's always given the best hugs, and I melt into it. My breath hitches. I've had the same plan for so long. I have no idea what I'm supposed to do now that it appears to have changed.

A knock at the window startles both of us. Doris is standing outside, shivering in her pajamas and looking terrified. She'd taken the day off from school, using one of her two allotted mental health days for the semester to skip the last day. I would have done the same if not for taking off on Monday.

Dad opens the door. "What's up?" he asks.

"I just wanted you both to know that I'm a boy and my name is Dylan and you can't do anything about it." The words are so fast that it takes my mind a moment to catch up. My sibling about to turn and run, but Dad grabs the person who is apparently my brother into a hug.

His strange behavior from the past few months comes into sharp perspective. The clothes. The constant search for approval.

I have a brother.

"Okay," Dad says. Dylan's eyes are rimmed with red, and a sob bursts out of him.

"I think I need a nap," I say. "It's been a big day."

Dad shakes his head. "That's too bad. We need to take Dylan to get new clothes and a haircut, then we're having a family pizza night. Mandatory."

Dylan beams, tears streaming down his face.

Things are going to be okay.

Chapter Thirty-Nine
Theo

I'M CURLED UP IN MY BED WATCHING A movie on Amazon when a call comes through.

Dad.

I hesitate, but after a few moments of deliberation, I answer.

"Hello?" I ask, my voice small.

There's a moment of silence then, carefully, a voice I haven't heard in months says, "Theo?"

Tears prick at my eyes, and my heart races. "Yeah, Dad. It's me." I try to sound casual, but I'm definitely not pulling it off.

He sighs, but he doesn't respond. I sit up, leaning against the headboard. I tap my fingers against my knees, sparks flying out. Luckily, they don't singe the vintage spread.

"What's up?" I ask, trying to sound casual and failing miserably. The thickness of my voice is obvious.

Another pause. "I got your acceptance letter to NYU. I guess they didn't get a change of address for you."

I bite my lip. I should be excited. This has been my dream for years. "Oh." After a much longer break in between words, I ask, "Is that all?"

He hesitates, but there's clear static through the line. The call hasn't been dropped, he just doesn't have the right words to say. Instead of speaking, I wait. The waiting is the worst part. I've been waiting for months.

"I thought you should know that I've been seeing a therapist," he says. "He told me that I should call you, but I've been too afraid." He stops, then starts again. "I thought the letter was a sign."

I look down. I should be crying, but the tears have all dried up. A hollowness fills my chest.

"Well thanks for letting me know," I say. I'm not sure how else to respond.

"I was thinking that you could come back," he says. "After you graduate. You could move back into the apartment for the school year." He pauses once again. "If that's what you want."

I pick at some dirt under one of my fingernails. "Maybe. I mean, I'll think about it. I have to go, though. Talk to you later?" The last word betrays my true emotions, cracking my facade into a million pieces.

Dad says, "I'll call you tomorrow."

I can't get my hopes up, but I smile just a little. "Talk to you then," I say.

"Love you," he replies.

I pause. "Love you too."

When I hang up, Mom knocks on the door and lets herself in.

"Was that your Dad?" she asks gently. I stare at my phone and nod. The whole conversation is still making its way through my head. "How are you feeling?"

I look at her. "Did you know Dad gave me a

credit card before we left? I only used it once, but I have it."

Mom raises her eyebrows. Apparently this is not something she was made aware of. My hands spark, and she looks down. "Have you been practicing your astrapomancy?" She rushes over and takes my hands in hers. The backs of my hands are lined with marks that look like lightning frozen in time. "You're not supposed to go without practicing. It can be dangerous for you." Why does she sound hurt? Or is it concern? I turn away and tuck my hands into my armpits so she can't evaluate them anymore.

"Dad wants me to live with him while I'm at NYU," I say to change the subject. "It might be a good idea. I wouldn't have to pay for a dorm that way."

Mom nods, her face grave. "Alright…" She stands and goes to look out the window, arms crossed. "Is that something you want?"

I sigh with frustration. "I don't know. I have no idea what I want. Everything is so complicated right now, and I have to go to court tomorrow because someone tried to kill me. It's kind of impossible to think about this stuff."

Mom doesn't respond for a moment. When she does, her words aren't what I expect. "I was thinking that you should see a therapist. It's something I should have done after the incident at the parade, but you seemed so...fine. But I should have seen that you weren't."

I look away from her.

"I have an appointment for you next week."

I stand up and go to her. When did I get taller than my mother? She's so much smaller than me, practically brittle. I wrap my arms around her and rest my head on her shoulder. "That seems like a good idea."

Epilogue
Billie

I SHOVE THE LAST OF THE BAGS INTO THE backseat of the car, slamming the door over it. The trunk and backseat are filled to the brim. How do I own so much crap?

"That's the last of it!" I call before Theo can make her way back into the house. She'd only had two suitcases full of stuff. Maybe I should try that minimalist thing that she's been getting really into this summer since graduation.

Dad comes over and stands in front of me awkwardly. "You've got your phone?" he asks, and I hold it up to show him. "And cash for the tolls?"

I laugh. "Yes, Dad. We have everything we need."

He runs a hand through his hair and looks away. Dylan is sitting on the porch, sulking because Dad wouldn't buy him concert tickets for next month. He's only thirteen, and he wanted to go alone. "Remember, if you get tired, take a break," Dad says. His voice is thick with emotion.

I wrap my arms around him. "It's gonna be okay, Dad. Dylan has assured me that he'll be as much of a goblin as possible to make up for my absence."

"Gee, thanks," Dad says with a chuckle, but when he pulls away, his eyes are red and wet. He sniffs.

"I love you, Dad," I say. "And I'm gonna see you for fall break, Thanksgiving, and winter break. It'll be like I never left."

He nods but looks up to keep the tears in his eyes. I laugh and hug him one more time. When he releases me, Theo is by the driver door of the brand new Honda her dad bought her for her birthday—apparently, her mom had vetoed a Mercedes. "Ready to go?" she asks gently. Her parting with her mom and Nana had been equally as emotional.

I look back to Dad, then nod.

"Be good," I call to Dylan, and he flips me off while Dad's back is turned. What a little asshole. I return the favor, and he smiles. He starts his last year of middle school before high school next week, but it seems like he'll do fine. At least he's strong.

I climb into the car, and Dad gives me a kiss on the forehead before closing the door for me. As we drive away, I watch in the mirror as he stands in the driveway until I'm out of sight.

When we turn onto the interstate, leaving Bore's Grove behind, Theo takes my hand.

"Ready?" she asks, her voice riddled with nerves.

I squeeze back. "Ready."

KATE HALL is a full time traveler, dog owner, artist, wife, and reader. She believes in wild things like love, magic, and basic human decency. Some of her least favorite things include selfish people, eating fish, and tornados. *Smoke and Mist* is her first novel.

www.KateHallBooks.com

Twitter @KateHallAuthor

Instagram @KateHallAuthor

Books By Kate Hall

From the world of THE ACADEMY:
Smoke and Mist
Ignite the Mountain

ANGEL ACADEMY
Angel Academy
Clandestine Angel
Renegade Angel

GINGER HILLS
The Girl in the Lake
The Girl Who Won't Drown
The Girls Down Below

VAMPIRE HUNTER CHRONICLES
Night Academy
Deadly Academy
Final Academy

SOUTHERN WITCHES
Southern Charms
Southern Spells
Southern Neromancy

www.ingramcontent.com/pod-product-compliance
Lightning Source LLC
Chambersburg PA
CBHW020605180626
46810CB00007B/2653